Call of the Penon
By
John Spencer

Call of the Penon

First published in the UK in 2024.

© Spencer Presentation Limited.

The right of John Spencer to be identified as the Author of this work has been asserted in accordance with the Copyright, Designs and Patents Act 1988.

All rights reserved. No part of this book may be reprinted or reproduced or utilised in any form or by any electronic, mechanical or other means, now known or hereafter invented, including photocopying and recording, or in any information storage or retrieval system, without the permission in writing from the Publisher.

Also by John Spencer

UFOs 1947 to 1987 published by Fortean Tomes

Phenomenon published by MacDonald & Co (Publishing) ltd

Perspectives published by MacDonald / Futura

The UFO Encyclopedia published by Headline plc

UFOs the Definitive Casebook published by Hamlyn

The Paranormal – a modern perspective published by Hamlyn

Gifts of the Gods published by Virgin

Prologue

Maria broke the stalemate. 'I've had it with you Steve. I'm going to the police. And if Mike comes to any harm, you'd better enjoy eating paella four times a day because I will make sure you go to prison. I will tell them everything.' She hesitated, trying to catch Mike's eye but he wouldn't take his eyes off Stephen. Finally, she turned and hurried off down the slope, and out of sight.

Stephen seemed to think about it for a while, then nodded, and stepped back aside again to let Mike pass. Mike could see that it would be easiest if Stephen went ahead, but he clearly wanted to force Mike into the vulnerable position. Mike looked around; there was no one else anywhere on their side of the Penon. Out of options and knowing he would have to hold on tight as fuck to the chains, Mike started to move. He was ready to push back if Stephen did attack but he desperately hoped that this was just an over-dramatisation that Stephen was enjoying and that it would soon be over. But he's still got the gun. The thought came unwillingly into his mind, he tried to push it back and focus just on the Penon.

Mike grabbed the first of the chains, holding on with a finger-numbing grip, and began to edge across.

Stephen moved closer, shaking, and Mike realised his mistake, he couldn't move his hands from the chain, couldn't do anything to stop Stephen if he decided to push him straight off the ledge.

Stephen levelled the gun towards Mike, and still Mike couldn't tell if it was a bluff or if he was willing to follow through.

Streatham 1979

Maria had spent over ten years in England and her language was perfect. Well, if not perfect then certainly a bloody sight better than most people's Spanish. Several times that feeling had built up inside her. She remembered once when she had been in a supermarket asking for something very ordinary – soup, she recalled – and her mind blanked on the word. It must have happened to lots of people, even those for whom English was their first language, but she tried to get the point across by saying 'sopa'. The woman she was speaking to threw her hands in the air and walked away saying if she couldn't speak English she should 'piss off out of my country'. Even knowing that it was the assistant who was at fault didn't help Maria's embarrassment or stop her feeling in some way inadequate. Whenever anything like that happened her friends told her to be strong, to ignore it, and reminded her that most English people cannot speak any other languages half as well as she could. But it rattled, and she knew it probably always would.

She kicked herself every time she knew that it had led her to take a lesser job than she was capable of, and some mornings she had to throw her toothbrush at the mirror and then go and pick it up out of the wastebin before she got over it. To pay the rent on her former flat she had had to work in an extra job, and sometimes two extra jobs, to make ends meet. She had friends who constantly tried to buck her up, encouraged her to ask for more money or change jobs. And she always agreed that she would and then shouted 'mierda' - or 'fuck' - when she was on her own and had to get her toothbrush out of the bin again. Her employer paid other people more for the same work; they reassured her that this had nothing whatsoever to do with her nationality, or her language or her accent, and that there were other 'contributing factors'. The truth of course, and what kept her toothbrush sailing constantly through the air, was that it had everything to do with these things. The fuckers kept paying her less because they knew she couldn't ask for more.

Juliana also said 'fuck them' a lot and sometimes helped her get her toothbrush out of the bin. She was a friend who had tried so often to get Maria to change her attitude. 'You deserve better. They know it.

You know it. You should press them to up your pay.' Maria listened because she knew it was true, but she also knew that Juliana came from a different culture and couldn't always understand what she had never experienced. They had a good friendship, but it didn't work when Maria was alone in her flat. Or in her bathroom.

Juliana worked in a classy London shop and earned a far greater salary than Maria did, and probably, Maria reflected wryly, did a lot less work. Maria didn't talk about it with her, but suspected that that far greater salary was peanuts to her, the opposite of Maria's struggles for money.

'I know, I know,' Maria had said despondently last Friday. 'Jules – I know you're right, but I wouldn't be any happier if I lost my jobs either!'

Juliana felt the injustice of that, but she just nodded. As she had done a thousand times before.

Maria worked in an IT firm. She helped develop programs for their calculations and yet her work was labelled 'admin'. She sat in the works loo and cried sometimes, and swore often, at people who were given better titles and more money for the same work. She wasn't just fucking admin! Not actually swearing at them of course but swearing at their image in her mind on the loo. And then she would stand up, straighten her blouse, slam her hand on the door in frustration, and plaster the required smile on her face to agree with people and let them know that they were right, and they were wonderful.

But she didn't like the other jobs she had either, or one of them at least. She cleaned the offices of two nearby companies but she couldn't even start until they all left at eight or nine at night and so she often didn't get home until 'god-knows when' in the morning. For what they paid her she had to sit around waiting to work, unpaid, and then work late and more often than not get a taxi home because there were no buses or trains.

The other job was better; she taught yoga in a couple of local gyms. She had been doing yoga for many years and she jumped at the chance to make a little extra money teaching it to others.

It was there that she had first met Juliana who took her classes, and after a while Juliana had come to like Maria's style so much that she only took her classes. If Maria was absent for any reason, Juliana shied off from the group for that session. Over time Juliana and Maria became friends who could share more and more, and after a while they chatted freely.

Maria had qualified as a yoga teacher years ago and had considered making a career out of it. She constructed a series of gyms and studios in her mind where she could teach yoga full time, but they didn't ever materialise. The gyms took more and more of the money. They would book her, and commit her, but could cancel without warning or pay if they didn't get enough interest. She thought that the other trainers would feel the same injustice she did, but she soon discovered the money was just a bit extra for them; a paid hobby. She needed the money for rent, to heat her flat, and buy food. They just use the money for champagne to wash their teeth with! She knew that wasn't completely fair but it also didn't feel that far from the truth.

Life had started to look up a bit after she met Stephen. He was a regular at her yoga classes and she couldn't help smiling a bit when it came time to teach his class. She would forgo her usual outfit choice of 'whatever is on top of the pile' in favour of a more careful selection (not that she would admit that of course). She noticed him hanging back after class one week.

'I'm fairly new to yoga,' he told her, 'I'm enjoying your classes.'

'Thank you.'

'What's really good about you is that you don't force people to match your speed, or the speed of the others in the room. You let us all move at our own pace. I don't know how you do that, but it totally works for me.'

'Thank you. That's really nice to hear.' In secret, she agreed with him. Neither Susan or Tamsin – or any of the other trainers – were able to personalise their sessions as she did – but she bit back the words. 'The substitutes are all very good,' she had said to him. 'They'll still look after you.' She loyally remembered that she had been told to always boost the images of any of the trainers; she wondered if they all did the same for her.

Other times he stayed behind a bit longer than the others as they wound up their mats and put their blocks away, and he would take the chance to bid her goodbye each time. Then he slowed down his getting changed so that he would arrive in the café area of the gym when she got there.

'I love the yoga,' he told her. 'I wasn't sure I would when I first started but I'm really getting into it.' Eventually he asked her if she would like a coffee. 'Yes', she said immediately and then feared she had been too keen.

Coffee was nice, and their conversations were friendly and intelligent. Sometimes they were about nothing in particular, a lot of times they were about their work. 'When you were easing off with the 'boat pose' you had us all doing, the slow-down worked well for Elsie,' Stephen said.

'It was mainly for her I slowed us down. I could see it was tough for her. A couple of others behind you did more than I asked. I think it worked.'

He made a point to always ask if she was free and never assumed she would be. It made him seem gentle. A couple of times Juliana had spotted them together in the café, and she had always waved, smiled intimately to Maria, but left them both alone.

When Stephen asked her on a date he only got in just before she asked him. She wasn't letting him get away if she could avoid it, and she was delighted he had made the move. Their first real date was an invite to a film, which she decided to accept it whatever it was. She imagined there was a chance he would like something very different to her tastes, maybe a war film, or a gangster movie. She gritted her teeth a bit (invisibly, she hoped) when they approached a cinema proudly displaying 'The Amityville Horror' which she had read was very unpleasant. But they watched another film that had just been released, Superman, which although a high-action movie, turned out to have more romance than she expected, and, while not a comedy, it was light-hearted and fun to watch. She would never have chosen to go and see it, but she really enjoyed it, which made her feel that bit closer to Stephen.

They also went to the latest James Bond film which she was keen on. That had been her choice and she was delighted that he had gone along with it.

'Do you know that NASA are still fighting very hard to get their shuttle into space? The filmmakers wanted to get their film out, and their shuttle into space, before NASA actually did and they made it.' Stephen told her.

'How do you mean?'

'NASA rolled out its first space shuttle in 1976, though that was only a test vehicle that didn't go into space. They haven't actually got one into space even today. Could be another year or more.'

Maria was impressed that he had read around the subject. She also noticed that they laughed at all the same parts of the film. Maria didn't expect them to be identical, but she felt that they had a lot in common. They laughed a lot, chatted a lot, and enjoyed the fact that they seemed to have fairly similar views on politics and religion – neither of them having very strong opinions of either!

They would often have a snack, or even a quick meal, after the films, but it was when they had dinner that Maria felt that it was a 'proper' date. A booked restaurant, classier than the restaurants next to cinemas, and a good menu. It was the first time they had been to a restaurant where only Stephen's menu had prices on it which made her feel very adult, if patronised. They spent hours chatting over a host of things and afterwards she couldn't remember virtually anything they had talked about. But she knew they had enjoyed those hours so much and she went home feeling she was floating.

They had several dates of that kind and she started again to think something needed kicking into gear. She held herself back a bit, wondering if he would make the move first, but finally worked up the courage to invite him back to her flat for a coffee.

'I'd love to. I was hoping you'd ask.'

She smiled at him.

'If you hadn't,' he added, 'I was going to climb the window to your balcony and attract your attention like Romeo.'

'I don't have a balcony.'

Stephen grinned. 'Did you know that there was no balcony in the original play? The word didn't even exist at the time. It's just been done like that so many times in the theatre, people always think there has to be one.'

'I still don't have one,' she said, smiling.

'I would have thought of something.'

They went inside. As the door closed he kissed her hard and passionately. Within a fleeting time that night they were naked on the floor of her living room. (Later, after she insisted on hearing every last detail, Julianna commented, 'it sounds like you're putting those yoga skills to good use,' causing both of them to roll around the floor laughing).

Maria could see how good they were together, and she thought about them moving in together. She knew he was just renting a room in a house locally, and she assumed that they would discuss both giving up their places and finding a place of their own. That was when the first meteorite crashed through her wall.

'Let's do it. I'll move in here,' Stephen said. 'We can see how it works out and go from there. It'll be fun.'

Where was the discussion they were going to have? Weren't they going to decide how to move in together? And where?

Stephen left just after so she assumed they would discuss it next time they were together. That was her first serious surprise. That was when the next meteorite crashed through the wall and bounced off the sofa. Before she knew it and before they had even met up again he told her he had given up his room.

Juliana was taken aback when she was told. 'It seems like a big move, after only a small amount of time.' But Juliana thought Maria was smitten, and she decided it was best to let her rise or fall her own way, and said nothing else.

'Stephen?' Maria stood at the door, when she opened it to a knock, looking at Stephen standing there. He said nothing, but she could see two roughly packed suitcases and a rucksack sitting in her hallway. Fucking hell! They were looking at each other across her doorway and there was Stephen and all his goods standing there homeless.

'That's still okay with you?' he checked. 'No' was the answer screaming around in her head, but how do you say no to a homeless friend standing on your landing? Standing with his boxes and bags all over her hallway. She thought she should say something, should establish her own territory, but he was already carrying boxes in past her. Maybe it would be fine, she told herself. So she agreed with him that this made it easy. She was keen to have him with her, and she knew that there was nothing wrong with the way it had happened. Nothing except that the way it had happened was, well, pissing wrong.

They talked about how to layout the place to suit them both, and they seemed to find all sorts of clever ways to make the space work for them. He always seemed to listen carefully to her wishes (and she would always agree later that, yes, he did listen well) but sometimes (all the time!) they seemed to settle on what he had wanted to start with and she would be nodding along a bit lost in his unwavering sureness that yes, it probably did make sense that he would need space for a desk and yes of course she could use the gym if she wanted to keep up with her yoga.

He didn't understand why she kept throwing her toothbrush around the bathroom.

Cycling came out of the blue just a few weeks after Stephen had moved in.

Her time with Stephen was generally pretty good and she enjoyed it, albeit with a sense that in her own home she had become secondary. But in the gym she was still somewhere up at the top. One of her students joked that she was the gym's Brian Clough. When she asked who he was the student explained that he once described himself as 'not the best English football manager but somewhere in the top one!' She found that both funny and very complimentary.

As she worked on she realised that the spinning classes – on fixed gym bikes – were becoming very popular. Over a few months they went from being half full in many classes, to always full and often listing waiting lists of people hoping to get on if there were cancellations. She ran some of the classes and when she started getting asked if she could 'bump up' the activity to a tougher work-out she wanted to know why. At first she changed the work-outs to possibly tougher groups, but also explained that she had to keep the classes available for all members, including those that didn't want the extra.

Over a short while more she discovered that many of the members were working out towards a challenge they were signed up for. A group of members of the gym had signed up for a long charity cycle ride and they were looking for volunteers to join them. One of them was Mike, a regular at the gym whom she had spoken to a couple of times, and she chose him to find out more about the ride.

'What is it? How long is it?' Maria asked.

'About two hundred miles.'

She was a bit shocked. 'Shit. That's a hell of a distance. How long will it take?'

'Four days. Three days of cycling. It's about sixty or seventy miles a day. We get one day off to rest. It's challenging.'

She wasn't sure what to say.

'Have you done much cycling?'

Maria faltered for a moment, wondering quite what she should say. She wanted to volunteer for the ride, but had to admit she was hardly the right person for it. The gym trainees would expect her to be well prepared for the ride because she constantly trained them, several times a week, and they were used to following her instructions. But there was a catch she wasn't sure whether she should admit or not. But Mike was always friendly, and she thought that it was possible he would support her, even keep her secret if she shared it with him.

'Not so much lately but I used to cycle a lot,' she started cautiously. 'I can build up again.'

They were happy to get her on board the team, so she signed herself up. She felt a little thrill at her hasty decision and decided that no matter what Stephen might say (she wasn't sure why that thought had come into her head) she was going on that ride. But she had to share her secret with someone and she knew that someone was going to be Mike.

'I haven't got a bike.'

'That's easy. I can help you choose one if that's what you need.'

Maria took a deep breath and dived fully into the secret. 'It's a bit more than that. You know I told them that I used to cycle a lot. Well, I've never cycled in my life. Well, I cycled as a child, but not for years. Never as an adult.'

Mike said nothing. He was trying to work out if he was the recipient of a joke, or if she really meant it. Maria could see that plainly written on his face. 'I'm serious,' she said. 'I might do all this spinning stuff, but I've never really ridden a bike since I was a kid.'

Mike smiled. 'You've thrown away your stabilisers though?' The cheeky look on Mike's face made her laugh. She punched him gently and smiled and they laughed some more.

But the nerves were creeping in. 'Maybe I've gone too far. I've only got three months to train for this. I think I should tell them I can't join them. I can make an excuse.'

'You should do it. You can train for that in three months. You're well fit. You'll pick it up in no time. And you seem very determined. Just say you're going to do it, and you will.'

Maria lit up a bit as he said that; she enjoyed the sense of purpose she felt from it.

'Do you want help?' Mike asked her.

'Yes. Could you help me? I'm not even sure what I need.'

Mike thought about that for a bit. As he thought about it the list got longer, so he decided to keep it to himself. 'I think we should start at the beginning. Let's see what you can do. Once we've got you a bike, let's go out together and see how easy you find it. But bear in mind; whatever you feel at first it will get better.'

'I've got good legs,' she said. And she pulled herself up in case he took that wrongly. 'I mean fit, strong legs.'

Mike smiled at the slip. 'You'll need them. And by the time you're three hundred miles along the road you'll also have a sore arse, backache and probably aching shoulders. Cycling is a lot more than just pedalling. And you'll need creams as much as spare inner tubes.'

'Creams?'

Mike smiled. 'We'll get to that later. What about a bike? Can you borrow one or do you want me to help you get one?'

'I'd be really grateful. But I'm putting a lot your way. It sounds like I'm asking a lot of you.'

'It'll be a pleasure.'

Maria was troubled by the thought of the ride, but also excited. What she was less excited about, and more troubled about, was telling Stephen. She felt he would be against it, even if she couldn't say why.

That evening she prepared a lovely meal. He liked chicken; she bought one and prepared the best sauces and vegetables she could think of. Japanese sweet potatoes, tempura batter and tasty extras. Delia Smith was all over her kitchen that night!

When Stephen came home he was smiling. 'At work today I had a great time,' he started. 'Two new contracts I've been working on for new insurance programs both came in today. And one that I wasn't sure might happen looks strongly like it will.' Stephen and Maria rarely talked about his work which she barely understood, but she could feel his pleasure. The two of them slipped into an easy and happy evening, which Stephen felt even better about when the meal came out, along with a couple of beers.

Maria said that she was going to have a quick bath, but Stephen told her to wait for a few minutes and he would run the bath for her. When she went into the bathroom there were candles all around, and small plastic floats containing pretty flowers. She was delighted. Stephen could be thoughtless sometimes, but other times he came up with the most wonderful presentations.

'I have a surprise,' Maria told Stephen as they finished their meal. She felt, and sounded, nervous.

'Go on.' Stephen smiled and opened his hands.

'I've signed up for a bike ride. It's a gym thing, I'm just one of many.'

'Sounds good. When is it, after gym one evening, or at the weekend.'

'Well,' she said, edgily, 'It's a bit bigger than that. It takes four days. It's quite an exciting thing really.' She smiled widely, if nervously.

Stephen raised his eyebrows but didn't say anything. They were both silent for a while.

'What do you think of that?' Maria asked.

'I don't feel easy about it. It makes me feel strange.'

'Why? I'll be safe with plenty of others around me.'

'Do you know any of them?' Stephen was holding back. Maria stayed quiet and eventually Stephen added. 'Any of them, personally?' She could hear the acid that had crept into his voice.

' I know a few of them, but none, as you put it, personally. Why do you distrust me so much? You seem to constantly want to check on me. There's no-one I want but you. You know that.'

'Where are you going?'

'Amsterdam. It's for charity. It's a big thing the gym have backed and I want to be part of it.'

'Amsterdam! Good god.' Stephen tried to calm down and said, 'Four days is a long time.' Stephen banged his fist on the desk. 'No. It's not right. I'm asking you not to go.'

Maria could see the anger in him. Perhaps it included frustration, or fear, but it was certainly anger.

'I want to go.' Maria didn't know where her defiance came from, but as she said it she recognised something forming in her. She did want to go and, in that moment, she resolved that she would.

'I'm not getting much say in this,' Stephen said. 'This is all about you.'

'Some things are about us and some things are about you,' Maria said. 'And some things are about me. This is about me.'

Stephen didn't say much for the rest of that evening. Maria felt his anger again; he was grumpy and moody, and she could feel that he couldn't get out of it. Maria kept coaxing him, and eventually he seemed able to discuss it more cleanly.

'Why do you need to be away from me?'

'I don't need to be away from you. I just need to do this, to prove something to myself about what I can do. This is going to be a tough ride, and I want to look backwards on it with pride in years to come.'

Stephen said nothing.

'Is that so wrong?' Maria asked. 'Is it?'

They had mutually moved away from that argument that evening, but it arose again just two nights later. The night in between had been tense, with Stephen avoiding all of Maria's attempts at peace-making. But the following evening it blew up again and Stephen seemed to be sure he would talk her out of it.

'Is this about you going with someone else?' was his poker-hot stab.

'No. I'll be going with lots of people, but no one special.'

'Why would I believe that?'

Maria smashed the cup she had been holding onto the floor and looked him straight in the eyes. 'If I wanted an affair do you think I'd have to cycle to Amsterdam to get it? People have fucking affairs with their neighbours. I'm with you because I want to be with you. Get it Steve. Fucking get it.'

Stephen was on the back foot. He started trying to calm her down. He held her and they cuddled a bit, for the first time in a few days.

'What am I supposed to do while you're away?' Stephen asked. Maria could see he really was trying to get calm about it.

She smiled, and then laughed. 'Feet up on the sofa, Chinese takeaways every night. Ignoring the washing up. You can be a bachelor for a few days. Try to see the positive in this.'

And he laughed too, but it was tense and strained.

They had a few other rows over the next few days, but Stephen seemed really to be getting it together. He asked why he was not invited, and bristled a bit when she said it was a gym thing and he would feel like an outsider. 'So there are no couples going?' he asked.

'There are two or three but they're couples who regularly go to the gym together. You wouldn't know anybody there. This is something for me. Let me just do it.'

Stephen seemed to feel that he had no arguments left. And he felt that Maria had pushed the envelope too far – if he pressed she could leave him. Better, he thought, to let it happen and then pick up the pieces afterwards. Hopefully not too many pieces.

The smells of the Common came first; a sweetness of wet grass and a vague smell of flowers around the two small lakes on the edge. Mike arrived and unpacked the bike, fitted it out with water, spares, checked the contents of the travel bag and propped it up against a tree. He could see a few younger kids not far away who were watching him, and one stuck his tongue out. He smiled and stuck his out in return. He slipped on his cycling jacket and put his gloves and helmet down next to the bike. Maria arrived shortly afterwards, drove up and parked. He helped her get her new bike they had chosen together off the rack on the back of her car and waited as she put on her waterproofs and warm clothes.

'Let's get started,' Mike said.

'Just a slow trip round the park,' she reminded him. They'd agreed to first just make sure she had some balance, and some manoeuvrability. They slowly circled around the paths, and Mike watched as Maria felt her way. She wobbled a bit at first, almost brought the bike down too, but then found her rhythm; her balance improved, and she seemed to adjust her pace easily. She took the curves with ease, and in no time they got into a proper run.

'Just out of here. Through the town, heading up north. Then over towards the motorway, cut off just before it, and we take the A road back down here. That should be about ten miles or so. We'll give ourselves an hour and that should be enough.'

Mike couldn't help admiring Maria's form as much as he concentrated on her cycling. He followed along, sharing his mind between her technique and her curves. She had never ridden a bike on a road before; all her cycling was from the hours spent spinning in the gym. Although she was fit from all her exercise, she'd never ridden a bike much before at all. Halfway round, Mike overtook her and came to a halt, with her stopping just behind him.

They stopped at a water fountain. 'Have some water,' he suggested, taking some himself.

'How am I doing?'

'Good. Very good. You need to keep a little closer to the kerb, but not too close. Don't let your pedals hit the kerb. You need to dominate the road and not let cars push you around. At the same time, you need to let them pass easily. Say between half a metre and a metre from the kerb.'

She nodded.

'Apart from that no comments. Brakes feel okay?'

'Yup. Steering is comfortable. I feel good.'

'Wonderful. Let's go on.'

Mike would have been happy to finish the ride in an hour so he was whooping that they got there in only fifty minutes, and when they stopped she was breathing easily.

'Everything I've got is aching,' she said with a grim smile. 'And a few things I didn't even know I had.'

'You can't do anything for the first time without stretching a few new muscles.'

As they put the bikes away, hers back on her rack and Mike's in the back of his car, they chatted about how good it had been and how positive about it she felt.

'Next weekend good for you?' Mike asked her.

'If that's good for you too. You sure I'm not bothering you?'

'I cycle most weekends anyway. It's nice to have someone to talk to. Twenty miles next one? Give ourselves two hours? That okay for you?'

'I'll be here.'

Netherlands 1979

'You have to get it right,' Stephen remarked as they packed the car. 'You can't hop back from Amsterdam to pick up what you forgot.' Maria had asked him for help, hoping that by including him he wouldn't feel as put out by the trip as he had seemed to, but she was wishing she hadn't. His bad mood was making her feel edgy though and she was trying hard not to snap at him.

'If I'm in Amsterdam then I'll just have to deal with it; there'll be no problems.'

'You know what I mean.'

She nodded, not wanting to spoil their goodbye before the trip. 'I know. I've got my overnight bag with clothes, washing stuff. And plenty of warm layers in case it gets cold which it can do over there. And I've got my day bag which has some nuts and chocolate, drinks, and a couple of extra layers for the bike in case I need them. And the spares and kit for bike. '

'You need more stuff in the main bag.'

'There's no room. It's the biggest bag I can take, and I can only take one.'

'That's stupid. You're going over on a ferry, not an aeroplane. Another bag would make no difference.'

Maria thought about explaining what would happen if all forty or so people took an extra bag, or even two extra bags, but she couldn't get into the argument. 'That's the rules,' was all she said.

Lastly, they loaded the bike onto the rack.

After one final check, they climbed into the car and Stephen drove up to the hotel in Stanstead, parked and unloaded the bike and the bags. The first day of cycling would take them to Harwich from where they would catch the ferry. Most of the other forty or so people were there unloading bikes, fiddling with bikes, adjusting seats and so on. Stephen immediately felt like an outsider in a closed group; it was a feeling he hated and a feeling he had had many times in his life. He had an irrational thought that he should propose to her then and there, but he recognised it as a silly idea, a desperate idea, and he dismissed it.

That feeling was one he could remember even in early childhood. He was often included with other children, and they seemed genuinely to embrace him, but he always held something back. He wished even then that he could let it go, but he always kept some part of him to himself. And others felt it - he knew that - so they kept their distance just slightly. His mother had told him once that he shouldn't do that – 'You'll have no friends if you do that,' she warned him. And he knew, though he never openly admitted it, that she was right. But he couldn't stop it. Once or twice he really did let go and he really saw the difference it made, and he decided then and there that he wouldn't let it happen again. But it happened just the same the next time, and most times. He could remember once being with his parents at some adult's formal dinner of some sort – his mother's work's 'do' he thought – and he was told he could go in this other room to wait for a while. When he got in there it was occupied by four or five other kids playing happily and they immediately asked him to join in. But he was there just to wait for his parents, he remembered. So he just sat on a chair and waited. The other kids gave up with him and played together, and he waited. It had seemed like a lifetime of waiting, and when his mother came in to get him she just said 'Did you have a good time with the others?' And then he knew that he should have played with them, but he had thought he wasn't supposed to. He could remember the pain of that even now.

He needed to get into this group, he thought. 'You feel okay about this?' he asked Maria.

'You've hardly asked me that since we started. But, yes, I feel well prepared for it and keen to go.'

Stephen nodded. 'Good. Do you know all these other cyclists?'

'Not at all. I know four of them, I think. This is a general charity ride for the Cancer Group. Our gym crew is five, including me, but others are from other gyms and couple of charities.'

Stephen looked around. He had thought they were all gym crew but now he saw them differently, saw them as more varied.

'I need to get stuff sorted out with them. You be okay for a bit?' Maria asked.

'Sure. I'm going to just have a walk around. Is that okay?'

'That would be good. Give me time to sort things out.' She walked off to the small group of men standing together.

Stephen walked over to one man, surprisingly overweight he thought, who was unpacking a bike from a 'Halford's' box. 'Hi. This looks very exciting,' he said. 'Is it a new bike?' Stephen pointed at the bike coming out of the box. 'A new bike especially for the ride?'

'Not that simple. I've never really ridden a bike before. A friend lent me his bike for a couple of trial runs and so that I could check if I was in shape enough for the next few days. But this is my first bike. I bought it two days ago.'

'And you're literally unpacking it here and now ready for the ride in ... what? ... an hour or so?'

'Yes.' The man looked completely confident, but he made gestures like he had more work to do. Stephen wished him well and moved on.

Several others looked like experienced bike riders, such as the couple who talked about their cycling every weekend. One woman looked less experienced and when Stephen asked her if she was ready she claimed she was and said she had been training around Richmond Park for several weeks. Stephen thought about Richmond Park, a largely flat surface in a sheltered area. Again, he wondered if she knew what she was getting into. Because he hardly did himself. He wandered back to Maria.

'Some people here seem a bit naïve about this ride, are you sure it's a good idea?'

Maria was unimpressed. 'They all look fairly young. Young-ish anyway. I'm sure it will be fine.'

'Probably. I imagine everyone will get there. Some may be in better shape than others. But I guess you'll all get there in the end.'

'There's a van following us with snacks and drinks and I imagine that if anyone gets into trouble it would pick them up and look after them.' Maria breathed deeply, trying to hold back her impatience. 'Apparently there is always a bit of a mix. Anyway I've been training for months so I know what I'm getting in for.' She looked at Stephen but, if anything, he seemed more tense; he was looking around at the other cyclists critically.

Stephen wondered if her confidence had come from her training, or whether she was acquiring it from her gym friends. He felt a not-quite understandable pang touch him.

Over the course of the next hour or so, Stephen felt more and more pushed aside. First the gym team grouped together and discussed their tactics, if you could call it that. He stayed near Maria, but felt himself outside their group again, and knew that if he stepped away she wouldn't notice.

He felt himself sitting in that room at his mother's dinner so many years ago.

The group turned to face the team leader from the charity and he chatted through the rules, explaining how they could ride without getting lost despite having no markers directing them on the journey. ' I will be at the front and I will stop every now and again and make sure you are all with us. At each stop I will allocate one of you to be the back marker, so you will only leave that point when you know all the group has left. And you will stay behind the group at the back until we all meet up again and do it again. Clear?'

Everyone said, or nodded, that it was.

Then he summoned everyone to get on their bikes and get ready.

Stephen backed away, waiting to see if Maria would say goodbye. But all she did was break off from talking to her gym crew, waved to him once, and then the whole troop cycled off across the car park, out of the exit, and down the road.

Stephen stood there for a bit, then walked to his car and punched the door hard, putting a small dent in it. He added 'Fuck!' Then he got quietly back in his car and drove off in the opposite direction.

Maria stayed with the other cyclists for a while but soon they all split up and fell into various positions. Some were fast and seemed to be intent on keeping near the front, some cruised along easily but had to keep accelerating to catch up. Most jockeyed around the middle. Soon, Maria was assigned to be 'last in line' and Mike offered to stay with her.

Mike and Maria had stayed apart during the session in the car park.

'Thank you,' Maria said as they cycled together. 'Thank you for keeping back while I was dealing with Steve.'

Mike nodded. 'No worries. I'm sure he'll miss you over the next few days. Did you ever tell Stephen that you and I did the training together for this?' Mike asked.

Maria said nothing at first, and then smiled. 'Yes I did. But I just said you were one of several who helped me.'

'Not that I was the only one.'

'It seemed better to spread it round a bit. He is a bit ... possessive.' Maria thought back to some of those runs, even a couple that she had never mentioned to Stephen because he had been away and there had been no need to discuss it. She thought about their first fifty mile a day ride, and the impressive speed she had attained. How much she would have liked to share that success with Stephen, and how bitter she felt that she could not.

That first day proved to be a challenging, but satisfying, ride down to the port of Harwich. There, the bikes would be loaded onto the ferry to Hook of Holland and the cyclists would go to their cabins and spend the night resting while they took around six to seven hours to cross the North Sea.

It was a slightly hard ride; there seemed to be a lot of hills to be climbed. And Maria was also surprised that there were only short stops for snacks, even for lunch. It was explained to her that if you stop for too long your muscles cool off and it is harder to get going again. But she, and the whole crew, arrived at the dock in good time and in fairly good order.

On the ferry, Maria was in a cabin of three women and they chatted briefly but were quickly quiet. They could hear men nattering as they drifted off, and they slept deeply and restfully.

In the morning they were up early and straight to the onboard restaurant for breakfast.

The three girls sat together, having come down for breakfast together. 'Bit basic,' one of them commented at the small meal of eggs, one sausage and some beans. They bought some energy bars in the shop and all ate one as they finished their tea and coffee.

Maria managed to be one of the first to get off the ferry, hurrying so that she could get to a phone and call Stephen. This was the moment that Maria had been looking forward to. She had missed talking to him and felt a bit uneasy as she queued to use the dock's phone because of their tense parting the day before. 'Hi Steve. How are you?'

'I've been worrying about you. Is everything alright?' Stephen answered

'Yes, why were you worrying?'

'It's been ages since you called. Have you been distracted?'

'We just haven't had a chance to make phone calls. I had hoped to talk to you last night at the port but we had to board the boat.'

'You could have found the time before you got on.'

'We had a ton of things to do. I'm really sorry .'

'Well, I'm sure you tried.' Maria could hear how tense he was. She asked him if anything was wrong and could feel the falseness in his voice when he said 'no'.

Maria tried to jolt him out of his bad mood 'Well, the cycling yesterday was quite tough. Lots of hills. Weather not bad though. We're all looking forward to the rest of the ride though - no hills.'

'Is everyone else okay. You made any good friends?'

'I was in a cabin with two other girls last night. But we were so tired we fell asleep pretty quickly. They're nice girls though.'

'No-one else?'

'I've been sharing the back stop with a guy called Mike, the backstop means…'

'Mike?'

She regretted straightaway that she had mentioned his name. 'Yes. I got allocated to be a back stop quite early – I was proud of that – and Mike offered to share that with me.'

'Why?'

'Doing stuff together is better than being alone. He was just being friendly.' The laugh that came back down the phone was humourless. His comment 'Don't get too close to him. I might get jealous,' was just a bit desperate.

'Mike was one of the people who helped me train over the last few months. But there's nothing to make you jealous.'

'But he is a bit special then. You know him more than the others?'

'Not really. A few others who helped me are here as well,' she lied. She started to feel angry; she was lying where no lie should have been necessary. Stephen was forcing her down roads she didn't need to go down. 'I'm not getting that close to anyone,' she said lightly. 'What I want is to get back to you. I miss you.'

'I miss you too.'

She heard a bit more warmth in his voice, maybe she was worrying too much.

They left the port the next day and cycled north up the coast past The Hague, and immediately people were grunting and groaning or chasing each other when they could along some of the roads. Other times they could hardly move the bikes forward. They were using their gears as much as they would on a steep climb.

'You've been a bit unlucky,' the team leader shouted at their first stop. 'In a low-lying, flat country like this one, the wind coming in from the North Sea is the main thing that helps or hinders cyclists. Usually it is just a small difference but today it is fierce. You're going to have some tough times now and again.'

'This is harder work than I expected,' Maria said to Mike as they rode together, two or three others immediately with them. As they changed direction as the roads changed left and right, the winds could be with them or against them.

'He said the winds are strong. Perhaps they'll die down as we get inland.'

A third person called across. 'We don't go inland all day. I saw the maps earlier. We're pretty much going up the coast all the way. All day today.'

There was a general, slightly humorous, groan that went around the cyclists nearby. Basically, everyone was smiling though.

Mike got posted to the back and Maria cycled for a while on her own. It gave her time to think about the ride. She could feel the aches again, but much less than ever before; she felt she was becoming a 'real' cyclist, and she could feel a freshness in her skin and in her breathing that made her feel more alive. It had been hard work but she was fit and ready. She noticed that others were looking fatigued. She probably wasn't the fittest, but neither was she the least active. This ride was making her feel really good about herself. That helped her put Stephen into perspective; she damn-well would make him see that her success didn't have to depend on others, or take her from him.

Lunch was a pleasant stop, again a fairly short one, in good sunshine and in a clean and well organised place. They were in Scheveningen, a pretty little seaside town. They were all sitting in one room on long tables and benches which made it easy to chat and share their experiences of the ride together.

'I have two kids at home,' one of the group said. 'And being here is just wonderful. Don't get me wrong, I love my little tearaways but they take time and energy and by the end of most days there's not a lot left for me…'

'I know exactly what you mean,' another contributed. 'If it isn't cooking for them, or cleaning up after them, there's all the running about. And it's not just school, it's the trips after school and at weekends. Do you know my husband and I once worked out where the two of us took our kids one weekend and if we had been driving in a straight line we would have reached Scotland. Just trips around our town; but so many of them we would have reached Scotland.'

'But you probably had your husband's help?' one man along the table questioned.

'Yes, sort of. He did as I asked him but it's always us, the women, who have to plan the trips and get everything sorted. My husband does as I asked, but sometimes I do wish that he would do a bit of the prep work as well. It would be a nice treat to just jump in the car and do the driving for a change.'

There was a sort of silence, and Maria chipped in. 'I have a wonderful boyfriend. He helps me out a lot,' she said.

There was a general murmuring of praise and support.

'But,' Maria went on, 'a bit like you were saying,' Maria pointed across the table, 'I have to do all the planning and he does as I ask and I wish he would take some control.'

Grunts and cheers of support went out. Then a silence.

'Despite that, he's also so possessive. It's like he's frightened to let me out of his sight. I've never been with anyone else while we've been together, but it's like he thinks I'm looking for someone else every day.' There was no sound at all from the table. Maria didn't even notice that she had turned away from a light hearted banter into a darker region. 'Even coming here was a fight. I know he's worried I'm trying to get away from him, and even though I'm not, and won't, I'm going to get hell when I get back.'

'How do you mean 'get hell'?' one of the women asked quietly.

'Oh, nothing serious. Just moodiness and silence. It will last about a week and then die away. Until the next time.' Maria looked around the room; Mike was sitting on another table a little way away. She decided not to mention that she knew him and that he had helped train her; she assumed they would not understand and might even think there was something between them. Why in heaven's name couldn't you just tell the truth, why did you even have to lie to yourself? she thought.

'If my old man gives me hell he'll get a broom up his arse,' one of the woman said, and brought about peals of laughter. Maria joined in, glad to get away from the mood she had been in. She joined in the chatter and laughter until they left.

The end of that day's run was a youth hostel near Heiloo. It was basic but tidy, fresh and well-structured. There were two large dormitories, one for each gender.

'What's the hanky-panky going to be tonight?' one of the women asked the group.

There was a laugh. 'After that day in the saddle; no-one's getting anywhere near me,' another one said.

'I don't know how to chat up cyclists,' one girl said quietly 'or anyone else for that matter,' she added with a small laugh. Maria hadn't heard much from her, she thought her name was Samantha or Sally, and wondered if she would open up a bit more now that it was just the girls.

'Just let them see your sexy knickers,' was the suggestion made to her. Maria looked over at the other woman, Rosanna, who spoke loudly and looked around the group smiling broadly to see their reactions.

Samantha-or-Sally blushed. 'In these clothes the guys don't know what you're wearing,' she countered, smiling.

'They know darling,' was the reply. 'They know.'

Maria laughed with the group, but she wasn't that interested. She had her man at home, and suddenly she couldn't wait to be back with him.

The following morning, they made off along the road towards Edam and Volendam. They had started early so Maria hadn't managed to call from the port, and she was pleased the van had stopped near a phone booth. She grabbed a drink and then slipped away to make the call.

'Good morning gorgeous,' she started.

'You're late starting this morning,' was Stephen's first response.

'Good morning is also a good way to say hello,' she said. 'We got away about an hour ago but I figured it was too early to call you. We're on our first van stop.'

'I've been sitting up waiting for your call all fucking morning and you've just been cruising around on your bike. I've been worried about you. Why didn't you call me earlier?'

Maria was stunned, and hardly knew what to say. She had never heard Stephen swear quite like that. And why was he upset? She asked him that at least.

'I was worried about you. I've been up since early this morning thinking about you. It's not like I can just leave the house if I think you're going to call me.'

'Well, what could happen to me? If anything serious had happened you're my emergency number. You're the person they call to notify about me. If no one calls you, nothing has happened.'

'Maybe I wasn't your emergency call. You could have changed that overnight. How do I know?'

'What are you talking about? Who else would I want the call made to? Why…'

'I don't know what's going on with you, do I? You're with your gym friends, and other friends, how do I know if you've got a new special friend?'

Maria was getting stressed, and worse because she knew the stop would end soon and she might have to cut their talk off. 'You've got to be kidding me. I've been thinking about you all the time. Some of the girls talk about other guys, and I'm not part of that. I've got you. Why would I want anyone else?'

Something cracked in his mood and his voice softened. 'I'm sorry. I'm really sorry. I just had a bad night and a lot of weird thoughts. Sorry … Sorry.'

'Don't worry about it. I imagine it's hard being alone. But I'll be with you in a couple of days. Just remember that. And I'll need a rest when I get back…'

'A rest?'

'Well, I'm going to want to go straight to bed…'

'I'm going to make that bed really sweet for you.'

She felt he was still slightly on edge. Something in his voice… 'The team is getting keyed up …' she started.

'You've got to get going. I know. Call me again soon?'

'I'll call you when we stop for lunch, if I can find a phone.'

'Kay'

She felt nervous hanging up.

They rode off, her gym crew together, but it made her feel slightly uncomfortable so she dropped back to some of the girls and they rode on, chatting about the huge fields of tulips they were riding through. Mike rode up alongside her. 'You okay? Having a good time?'

'I really am, yes. I did worry a bit that I might have trouble with the cycling, but I'm dealing with it easily.'

'No aches and pains?'

Maria laughed. 'Plenty,' she said. 'But no more than anyone else and a lot less than some. I'm having a great time.' She waved her arm around her, 'And look at these flowers. It's like a rainbow all over the fields. I never imagined it would be so bright and colourful.'

'And scented. Can you smell it? Strong, beautiful smells.'

'Yes. You're right. The scents are as much as the visuals. It's an experience I never expected. At least not so vividly.'

They cycled together quietly for a while, occasionally making very small gestures to this or that part of the fields, and then Mike rode on faster and teamed up with a group of guys slightly ahead.

Maria rode alone. Other cyclists, groups of men and women, chatted on and off about the route, the layouts of the flowers, the weather and a host of other topics. Maria was only half thinking about the conversations; her mind was still muddled with Stephen.

Maria phoned Stephen at the next stop, but he was quiet and didn't chat for long. This was not the moment to get into a row. She nibbled the food, not feeling hungry and then spent the next hour-and-a-half cycling and hissing 'fuck' fairly quietly to herself, and feeling desperately hungry because she hadn't eaten.

They spent the afternoon on the last part of the run into Amsterdam.

The end of the ride was marked out to make a fun finale. They rode into the Vondelpark, and there was a string of ribbons hanging over a section with the words 'Finish Line' clearly displayed. There was a rush ahead of Maria as several of the fellows decided to make it a race at the end, and there was a lot of cheering and shouting as someone made it over the line first. Maria couldn't tell if it was one of her gym crew from where she was, but she was sure she'd hear about it later. Shortly afterwards she and a couple of the women crossed the finish line together and Maria joined in the whooping and cheering, feeling light and uplifted. She felt good that she had finished but also glad that she didn't have to do such hard work again, for a while at least. There was a part of her that wanted it to continue, but she was savvy enough to recognise that she wanted it to continue because that would delay the return to Stephen and the possible row.

They were served paper cups of wine and they all cheered each other for their success. There were a few people who looked a bit worse the wear for the three days, but everyone made it to the end which was wonderful.

They all collected up their bikes and loaded them onto a trailer van parked nearby as they were told to do. They picked up their day bags, and walked slowly, under direction, to the youth hostel where they would be staying the night.

Mike was walking his bike next to her. 'I think we're having a quick dinner, and then we're free for the evening after that,' he said. 'Do you have any plans?'

Maria wondered if she was being chatted up by Mike, even though he had not done that before. She found the idea pleasing even though she wasn't interested. She was with Stephen and she didn't intend to upset that. And Mike had to know that.

She dismissed the possibility whilst she also simultaneously dreamed that that was exactly what was happening. For a moment, an instance, she saw him undressed, and his naked body close against hers. She could feel him holding her tight, and hard, and kissing her in an almost brutal way. She could feel the shudder passing through her body, and for that moment she felt her whole body reacting to her fantasy.

She was about to answer when Mike held up his hands. 'Just friends. Nothing else. I know you have a guy back home and I'm not trying to interfere, but we've a night here and we should make the most of it. The innocent most of it. That's a Dawkins promise.'

'If that's a line it's a good one, but it's also correct.' Maria felt a sense of relief, if slight disappointment, as she came back to earth and put aside her dream. "And I just realised I had never heard your surname before. I like Dawkins.'

'Honestly, I know. Just friends.'

Maria nodded. 'What did you have in mind?'

'A bar maybe. Probably with some of the others. A few drinks that aren't off the back of a van with two wheels pushed up onto the pavement.'

'That sounds good.'

When they went into the youth hostel they first had the meal that had been laid out for them. Then they took their day bags to their beds and Maria saw that she had a choice; make the bed before going out or when they got back. On the bed was a plastic bag full of sheets and a pillow. She decided to deal with it immediately, and ripped open the bag, and quickly made the bed.

Maria showered, changed and went back into the lobby where she had arranged to meet Mike. He was sitting reading a magazine, and smiled when she arrived.

'Ready?'

'Yes. Do we know anywhere to go?'

'Some of the guys are going to a place nearby. Unpronounceable name but just around the corner from here. That suit you?'

Maria nodded cheerfully, and they walked together to a bar nearby. They passed a coffee shop, which blandly promoted cannabis for sale. It was apparent that although the people running the place were locals, most of the people buying the drugs were tourists.

'It's legal now over here,' Mike reassured her.

'Really?'

'Yes. Has been for a couple of years, I think. They legalised it. You can smoke it but you have to stay inside the coffee shops and not walk around the streets. I'm not quite sure about the details, but it's definitely legal now.'

Maria thought about it. 'Would you like to try some?' she said. She was shocked to hear herself say it; it was like hearing something revolutionary coming out of her grandmother's mouth. But she was excited even as she said it.

Mike stopped and looked in the window. 'Yes,' he said. 'Yes, I'd like to try it.'

'Do you smoke weed? Cannabis?' Maria asked.

'Never. You?'

Maria shook her head and walked on. But Mike had stopped and was looking in. He turned to Maria. 'If you're up for it, so am I. Let's give it a try.'

It was an instant moment of compulsion, but Maria was strangely proud that it had been HER moment of compulsion. They walked in together and she felt bold at having been the one to suggest it. And to have taken the lead.

There were a couple of other cyclists from the team in there, but they were people they hardly knew. They smiled and waved to each other, but Mike led Maria to another table, and they sat down.

They ordered coffees and they were cheerfully shown what was available on the counter. There were some complicated things, like a hookah, and some cakes that were laced with weed, so they were told.

But the simplest were a few euros for rolled cigarettes, called joints, and they bought two of those.

'A fair start,' Mike offered.

'Start? I wasn't planning to get crashed out of my head,' Maria warned.

'I think it would take more than that to crash either of us. Take a look around; no-one here looks that much affected by smoking it.'

Maria looked around and had to agree that no-one was looking drugged out of their heads. They sat down and lit up the joints and both, smiling, puffed on their first drag together. They looked into each other's eyes to see if there was any response to each other. But there wasn't and that caused them to laugh. They smoked their way through the two joints and then ordered a couple of glasses of wine. When the wine was finished Maria went back to the bar and came back, not with the promised two more glasses of wine but with two more joints.

She handed one to Mike, with a distinctly cheeky look on her face. 'You're up for another one?' she challenged.

Mike smiled and they slowly smoked through the second joints. Mike started trying, unsuccessfully, to blow smoke rings and each time he failed the two of them laughed louder.

They had a cup of coffee each and then left the bar. 'That was less effective than a glass of scotch,' Mike offered and the two of them seemed to find that so funny they chuckled virtually all the way back to the hostel.

At the hostel, Maria looked at Mike. 'Thank you,' she said.

'For what? Leading you to a criminal lifetime of pot smoking?'

'You said it's not criminal here. No, not that. Thank you for not trying it on.'

'Not chatting you up?'

'Yes.'

'Don't think I wouldn't. And don't think I didn't think about it. And I do mean that. But a promise is a promise. And I like you, genuinely. I wish you and your guy … Stephen you said? I wish you both well. Really do.'

'Like I said, thank you.' She kissed him very lightly on the cheek and they parted.

In the morning they met at breakfast. 'I have to tell you a story,' Mike said. They sat down together with trays of yoghurt and coffee. 'Did you make your bed before you went out last night?

35

'Yes. I didn't fancy it for after we got back.' Maria was a little puzzled.

'I should have too. I made it after I got back last night. That was a mistake.'

'Why?'

'The pot I think,' Mike said. 'I have to tell you. I got back last night, felt fine, unwrapped the sheets from the plastic bag, made my bed and got in. Out like a light. I was thinking that the pot hadn't affected me at all. But this morning I woke up sweating like I'd never done before. Literally dripping with sweat. I was sure the pot had done something serious to me. I could feel a real strain and heat all over my body … don't look concerned, it's an okay story … when I threw the covers off I discovered I'd made the bed perfectly and then got into it, inside the plastic bag. All night.'

They laughed together.

The van took them that morning to the dock down at the Hook of Holland where they waited for their ferry. Talk was reduced; the event was over and although there were a few talking about reunions, as you always get, they were all just looking forward to getting home and getting back to their lives.

Mike was chatting with some others, and Maria spent a lot of time with other gym crew. There was a lot of chat about the ride; 'I was surprised the wind was more difficult than the hills', 'lunch on the second day was tasteless', 'I could hear a squeaking on my bike the whole way and I thought it could break down', and so on.

Maria stepped out of it to call Stephen just before boarding the ferry. She made sure she had enough coins for the phone box. 'I'm on my way home.'

'I've missed you. I'm looking forward to seeing you.'

'I've missed you too. I love you.'

'I love you too. I've been waiting to tell you when you get in, but I'm glad I've said it now.'

'Are you going to pick me up at Harwich?'

'That's the plan.'

She told him when she expected to get in. 'Probably take a half hour or so to get all the bikes off and sorted out,' she added.

At Harwich there was a great deal of everyone saying goodbye and soon-to-be broken promises to meet up again soon. Then Maria pulled away and pushed her bike over to Stephen who was standing by his car. She kissed him hard on the lips and he responded.

They loaded the bike up, and got in the car and drive off. Stephen broke the silence, 'The other day…' he started.

'What other day?'

'I was probably a bit tense on the phone. Maybe a little stressed.'

'Oh, then. Forget it.'

'It bothers me. I've been thinking about it. I should've been more sensible.'

'Just forget it.'

'I worried that you were…, that you could have…, well, all these guys with you. You could've been attracted to them.'

'Are you never attracted to other women?'

'You know what I mean.'

'It doesn't matter how attractive anyone is. I'm your girlfriend. And don't tell me you never do. But that's it. I'm your girlfriend, and you're my boyfriend. We don't need anyone else. I don't want anyone else.'

Stephen wanted to ask who she might have been attracted to, but he knew that would be pushing it too far. He was sure that nothing would have happened, and it troubled him that he felt like something could have. A part of him saw it as protective, but another part of him saw it as cowardice and frightening. He wanted Maria so much, but he knew that he had a fault in him that was going to be a problem.

But he didn't intend to start that way. He wanted, really wanted, to show her that he would not be a problem. He didn't just want to show her, he wanted to actually be better. She was the best chance he had to be the man he wanted to be.

That following morning he made breakfast and served it to her in bed, complete with flowers and a heart on a card. He knew it was over the top, but it was as much a start for himself as for her. He even laughed when she laughed at the presentation.

'Are you trying to convince me that this is my new life? Are you bringing me breakfast in bed every morning?' Maria asked.

'Would you believe it if I said 'yes'?'

'Not in the slightest.'

'Thank God. But a breakfast or something like it every now and again. I'd really like that.'

'I could get you one now and again too,' she said.

'I was hoping you'd say that.'

He hopped into bed with her, and the two of them ate the early morning fry-up that they both enjoyed. Maria tickled Stephen, and he messily threw bits of bacon at her, and they both kissed and cuddled and decorated each other's faces with food. Maria felt the warmth of their laughter.

Stephen hoped he wasn't laying it on too thickly; he really, really wanted this to be genuine. He took time in that week to do some chores he usually left to her. And it truly felt good when he'd done some dusting and loaded the washing machine. She genuinely appreciated it, though he knew she would have some doubts. She might even think he was covering up some infidelity or something equally concerning, but she said nothing like that.

Although Maria appreciated his efforts there were downsides too, for her. The living room had been a special place for her when she had lived there alone; now it felt strange, more like Stephen's, and, she thought, more 'male'. Her bookshelves had been a particular pride for her and she had her books laid out just as she wanted them. He didn't move them of course; she had never seen him read more than a newspaper, but now her books were behind his books that he never even looked at, and computer stuff from his work she didn't understand or care about. Sometimes Stephen was very tidy, at other times glasses that should have been in the kitchen, empty bottles of beer that should have been in the bin, pens and notepads, were left strewn about. The TV had faced a point between chairs; now it pointed exactly to the chair he used, and he moaned if she moved it. The remote was on his chair, always. He had files he hardly ever used and they were always left on the stool where she sometimes used to put her paperwork. Now, her papers were on the floor and for some reason she felt tense whenever she wanted to use the stool. When she challenged him, no matter how gently, he told her she was imagining it. Two people were always going to be different to just one. They both just had to adjust. She wanted to argue, and the old problem came back again; she didn't quite feel she had the language. In the end she thought he was probably right; she had to learn to share the space that had once been hers and that would take some adjustment.

'Do you think this is right?' she later asked Juliana.

Juliana hesitated before responding. 'I think you and Stephen could be very good,' she started. 'But it does seem a bit like he's the one making the rules and it was your flat to begin with… I think you should be clearer about what you want.'

'I have been clear,' Maria defended. 'I have been fucking clear. But he ignores me.'

'What have you asked him to change?'

Maria thought for a while. 'Bedsheets,' she finally offered. 'I told him I wanted coloured bedsheets. I have a range of them in the cupboard and I used to love varying them from pinks and blues, to deeper colours, and so on. But he only likes white. He insists men don't sleep in coloured sheets. So we only ever have white now.'

'And you had white ones too?'

'I have a couple of sets but I had to go and get another couple just in case.'

'He got them or you got them?'

'I got them. You think he's going out shopping for bedsheets?!'

'Well, you could have at least made him go and get them if he wanted them.'

Maria just shook her head. Juliana picked up again. 'Tell him you want to have a coloured set now and again. Even just one in four or something.'

'I tried. It wasn't worth the argument.'

Juliana sat down and said nothing. After a moment Maria said 'Chores.'

'Chores?'

'Lately he's been doing a few of the chores around the house. And I've been grateful for that. I had hoped it was a sign that he was going to take some responsibility for them. He stopped doing them pretty soon after he started. When I asked him to do stuff he always did it, and I think he really was trying to make a change. But I asked him to pick up some chores without me telling him and he just didn't understand. He thinks it's all my job and I can ask him to help me; he doesn't see it as our job together.'

'A lot of men don't, to be fair. But I agree with you it works best when they do.'

'I want him to. But he really doesn't see it as what he should do.'

Maria said gently. 'Another problem I have is that I want to see my friends. But Stephen doesn't like me doing that.'

'Why not?'

Maria shook her head slowly. 'Actually I don't know. He's never said anything. He doesn't even say I shouldn't, but every time I do he's moody and grumpy and it's got to the point where I just avoid it rather than have a row.'

'What about when you see me?'

'I think he's more used to you. But even so I don't tell him if I can avoid it. He doesn't know I'm seeing you now.'

Maria took a drink and smiled directly at Juliana, but it was a forced smile. 'There is a lot of good too,' she said. 'We watch rubbish game shows on TV together and get out bottles of wine, drink to excess, and get pissed at least once a week and at those times we laugh, giggle, fall into sex. Times like that are really good, and they make the dodgy bits go away.'

Juliana nodded, also smiling.

'One time he was really good. On my birthday I just expected it to be more of the usual. I knew he'd get me a present, and maybe a card, and I thought we might have a meal in the evening – I'd be cooking it of course. But he was great. He gave me a really lovely necklace, I'll get it and show it to you in a minute, a really funny card, and then he booked us out for a meal. It was a very good restaurant, good food, and we got taxis there and back. And when we got back we had really good sex. Thoughtful sex on his part in fact. It was a great night.'

Juliana backed away a little thinking that Maria was getting into a very positive mood. She didn't want to start a row between them, and they had gotten to areas where she knew Maria had to be more forceful. She thought about her response for a while but Maria brought them some drinks and changed the mood. Juliana was happy to let it go at that time.

The sex was good. It was frequent and satisfying. He was a strong man, with a high sex drive. Was she imagining that there was less foreplay than before? But then a lot of her friends complained there was never enough of that, and increasingly when he had come he would pull out and end that time together. 'It's the difference between men and women,' one of her friends told her. One time when they laid back together she brought it up. 'That was lovely,' she started.

'Good.'

'I could have made it better perhaps,' she offered.

'It was great.'

'But I could have spent a bit longer at the beginning getting you warmed up.'

'Yes?'

'And you could have spent longer warming me up.'

'You didn't feel good about it?'

'It was great and I loved it. But everything can be improved.'

'You're thinking too much,' he said and got up and went to the loo. His not being there gave her the strength to carry on, shouting at the loo door.

'If we spent more time playing before you shag me we could both have longer and better sex.'

He came back in, obviously rattled. 'If you don't like sex with me, find someone else.'

He put on his top clothes, and stormed out slamming the door.

Later, Maria and Juliana chatted freely about many things, and at that time they were talking about Maria perhaps working at the shop with Juliana. It could be a significant change for Maria. Both of them were excited at the prospect.

But Maria had stopped talking in any detail to Juliana about her troubles with Stephen. She had never felt shy or hesitant to talk to Juliana, or other friends, but somehow she didn't want to now. Julianna always said how lucky she was when Maria told her about how Stephen had brought her little gifts or about those times he did lovely things. She didn't want to spoil it. She even thought that perhaps Juliana was holding some thoughts back, but it was better to leave that alone.

'I can hardly keep the place clean and tidy without your help,' Maria started one evening. 'I'd be grateful if you could do some stuff around the place.' To no response she added, 'More and more I feel I'm the one running this place.'

Steve looked up. 'How do you work that out? I figure I'm paying for most of this stuff.'

'Okay, you're paying for it. Some of it. But I'm doing all the work in it. You come home, have a few beers, and I'm doing all the cooking and cleaning.'.

He put his beer down on the table in front of him. He looked away from the TV. 'What do you want me to do?'

'Just the stuff that needs doing.' She waved her hands widely. 'Just stuff around the place.'

'Give me a list and I'll get to it.'

'There's no list. I don't get a list. No one gives me a list. Just do the things that need doing.'

He shook his head with a puzzled look. He looked around but could see nothing.

'Ironing. Cleaning. Dusting. Make some meals. You must have had to do those kind of chores where you lived before. How did you eat before?'

'Mostly out with friends. And some of that work is more your kind of stuff than mine. You've got to admit they're not the sort of things men do.'

Maria didn't know how to respond. She absolutely knew it was his job as much as hers. But how to tell him? It didn't occur to her that it wasn't her job to tell him. She thought about asking Juliana but added it mentally to the list of things she preferred to keep to herself.

But he was on another tack. 'I need to rest when I come in. My job is hard work start to finish. I want to rest when I get in.'

'I work too....'

'You don't work the hours I do. And your job doesn't push you hour by hour like mine does.'

'My work is hard too. You don't count the hours I spend in here cooking and cleaning as work, but it is. And It's hard work. And I have to do the yoga training to keep the money coming in as well.'

'Fair enough. But you've also given up the cleaning you used to do. That's my money that's made that possible. So, I think I need some payback on that. This is something we share. Each of us.'

She didn't know what to say to that. It was true that he was bringing in more than she was, but he was also keeping it. More of her money was going into the home, more of his was going into the pub.

'I need to see my friends and a lot of them go to the pub. It's a place to relax. And stop telling me what I can and can't do. You're becoming like a jailer trying to pin me down.'

'I don't want to pin you down. I want us both to have a good life and that means having a life with you, and some time with my friends and on my own. What's unreasonable about that?'

'I don't get any special time....'

'Yes you do. All the fucking time you're with your friends or down the pub or whatever. Where's my time like that?'

'You want to come to the pub with me? We go to the pub sometimes anyway....'

'I don't want to come to the fucking pub. I don't want to see you with your friends. I want you to have time alone and with them...'

'That's not a problem then.'

'But I want the same. I have friends and I hardly see them. Thanks to you.'

'I know some of your friends. Down the friggin' gym for one of them. They want to get you into bed and you think I should put up with that!'

'You have friends...'

'Men. Down the pub with male friends. You think they want to fuck me?'

'That's not what I mean. My friends are men and woman but they're not after me. We just have common interests.'

'Like cycling?'

'Yes, cycling. I've got more into that since I got back from Amsterdam. I go out in a team with them, men and women.'

'All the special ones, yes?'

'Mike is not special. You've gone on about him since I got back. I hardly see him.'

'I talked to one of your team when we down the gym the other night. She said you and Mike were together for the whole of that ride. And he spent loads of time with you before.'

'I didn't.....'

'Like fuck. I want you out of the gym. There's a million jobs you could have, and better paid than that too. You could get a good job, bring in a bit more money, and stop trying to get yourself laid.'

'Fuck off!'

Maria stormed out of the room, crying and sweating. She knew people had arguments, everyone does, but why this argument? Why was she always defending something she hadn't fucking done!

London 1982

Juliana and Maria drank early morning coffee together, getting ready for the day ahead. Two of the staff were outside, smoking round the back, which was forbidden in the shop itself; the two of them were in the kitchen area for their coffee and slice of toast. Maria had come to work with Juliana in Styl, an upmarket, expensive clothes shop in the King's Road, Chelsea, and dealt with an array of rich, famous and, mostly pretentious, customers. The shop opened at 10am – none of their customers, or clients as they had to refer to them, would have been around earlier than that – but all the staff tended to get in around an hour earlier to get the shop, and themselves, ready.

When Maria had asked Julianna if she could help her get a job in the shop she worked in they both thought it would be a chance to rekindle their friendship a bit, but Maria seemed more private now and Julianna wasn't sure how to break through. Maybe she had to accept they had grown apart. There had been other subtle changes; the old Maria had loved the gym and her yoga, but for ages now she had not been in the gym. Juliana wasn't sure what had changed. Maria had mumbled something about wanting more female company but Julianna wasn't convinced, it's not really any of my business she thought and sadly accepted the truth of that.

Juliana had been at the shop for a while and was well thought of. She was diligent, friendly, and did her best to get on with people. She didn't see the shop as a long-term career, but it gave her good money, had some exciting ups and downs, and provided the opportunity to enjoy London at its best.

'It's a nice day today, and a Saturday, could be busy,' said Josephine.' Josephine was the manager of the shop, who was paid a small fortune to keep the place running the way the owners wanted it, but who hardly ever turned up in the place. That was, apparently, not needed. 'Good to hear we have a new royal,' started Josephine. 'Prince William of Wales he'll be known as apparently'.

'Born just a few days ago. Unfortunately, he won't be a client of ours. Unless he comes to like cross-dressing.' Hannah said.

Hannah was an assistant who had joined the company over a year ago and managed to upset almost everyone working there, and who would have been sacked long ago were it not for the fact that virtually every client loved her. So often she said things that frightened Josephine into expecting criticism from her very special clients and so often she was applauded or laughed with, much to Josephine's surprise.

'Let's assume he won't,' said Josephine stuffily. Hannah shrugged and leaned back against the wall. 'I was thinking only this morning about Princess Diana coming in here just before her wedding last year. That was a very good period for us. I hope she will return soon. We still have just the fashion finery that she deserves.'

'I always thought there was something a bit weird about what Charlie said when they got engaged,' Hannah chipped in. 'Something strange there.'

'He is Prince Charles, Hannah,' replied Josephine. 'Never Charlie. And certainly never if he ever comes in here. What do you mean anyway?'

Hannah crossed her arms defensively. 'They asked them if they were in love and Diana said of course they were. And then he said something like 'whatever love means'. That's a strange thing to say anytime. Let alone when you're announcing your engagement to millions of people on tv.'

'Just caught him off guard I think', Josephine suggested. 'It must be hard to deal with pressures like they have to. Even so…'

'Well let me know if they break up,' Hanna said, laughing quietly, 'I'm still available.' After a pause Hanna checked around the room to make sure that Maria wasn't with them. Finding she must be outside, she added 'It also made me think about Maria.' She pointed to the closed door.

'Does she want to marry him too?' Juliana asked, laughing.

'I doubt it. She's with Stephen of course. Always a bit of a strange pair though.'

'Why?' Juliana looked directly to Hannah.

Hanna shook her head at first. 'He hardly ever comes to office dos. I've hardly ever met him.'

'So what?' asked Juliana. None of us bring our partners in that much.

'True, but we all know the partners to some degree. What does anyone here know about Maria's Stephen?'

'Maria hardly comes to anything herself so it's no surprise he doesn't come.'

Hannah wasn't giving up that easily. 'Does that not have a feel to it? I sometimes feel really sorry for her. I could be wrong but I'm sure that she would come to more if she could. I think Stephen stops her. Or discourages her anyway.'

Juliana just shrugged.

'I was listening to her on the phone a while back,' Hannah went on. 'She was trying to persuade him to come to one of our evening drinks and it ended up with her not even going herself. Like I say, I think he stops her.'

Juliana was thoughtful. 'She must have loved him, or she wouldn't have married him,' was all she offered out loud.

'Yes, I know.' Hanna thought for a bit. 'But you can make mistakes.'

They tidied up and got ready to open the shop. But Juliana had trouble getting that out of her head. It put into words what she had been thinking for some time. She knew Maria had problems in her marriage, but then didn't everybody? She had tried to talk it through with her years ago and she remembered backing off then in case she put her foot in it. Or both feet, in fact. And it was still there, and, what she hadn't quite realised, was that it was obvious to others. Hannah was as subtle as a train wreck, but probably others had sensed it too, but were more discrete in what they said.

She started to regret that she had not pursued it those years ago. Part of her said that it was not her business, which was true. But part of her knew that she had side-stepped it to make life easy for herself. She hoped she had not missed a vital moment that might never come again.

London 1982

It was later that same year that Juliana was talking to Maria about holidays.

'I'm thinking about somewhere in Europe this year,' Juliana said. 'Somewhere easy and quiet and peaceful.'

'And romantic?' Maria smiled indulgently.

'And romantic.' Juliana smiled back.

'Is that a revival with … what's his name? … Jock? Josh?'

'No, that died last year. I've been flying solo for a while.'

'Sounds like you now have a co-pilot you're thinking about.'

Juliana nodded slightly. 'He's a new guy, but he's a good one. I'd like to see how he works out.'

'A keeper?'

'Oh, too early to think like that. But a maybe, I'd say.'

'It's not that guy you went to the theatre with a few weeks ago , is it?'

'Yes. How did you know? Have I mentioned him?'

'A few times but I didn't realise it was serious. I'm just excited for you.'

Juliana looked very happy. Maria asked 'How did you meet?'

'In the gym. He's been there a while. There's a lot of us that do the same work-outs, and some of the same classes, and … well, the usual stuff. We did a few work-outs together, had a few coffees together, and eventually went out a couple of times. He's really nice.'

They chatted for a bit about the gym, and about Juliana's other interests. Eventually it led back to the question of holidays.

'Sounds lovely. And now you want to go on holiday with him?'

'Yes. We've had a few weekends away and I think a holiday would be good. Somewhere easy and lazy and where we can spend some time together.'

'What's his name?'

'Mike.'

'And where would he like to be? Have you talked it through together?' Maria sat down and put her arms behind her head to relax her neck muscles. 'So, what's on your mind? Italy? Greece? Spain? Somewhere a little more exotic? An island perhaps?'

'I was thinking Italy. It has a range of lovely places that I'd love to see. Sicily and Mount Etna for one. Rome, of course, but that could be a bit busy. And that famous bay I can't remember the name of.'

'I'm guessing you mean Napoli?'

'That's it. Napoli. Some friends went there and they didn't even have to hire a car, they used local trains to get everywhere easily and cheaply. Pompeii and that other place that got wiped out by Vesuvius. And Vesuvius itself of course. If not though, and if we wanted to avoid Rome, there's still Florence and Pisa. Italy is just full of places that would be fantastic.'

'I would stick with Napoli,' said Maria. 'If you want to do Florence, or Rome for that matter, then you'd be better spending time just there. They're both full of good things to see, and both good places to have a relaxing time. Pisa, I must admit, is only worth a few hours and it's not too near anywhere else that's easy to get to.'

Juliana clapped her hands happily. 'I think you've persuaded me.'

'What about the boyfriend? Mike? Will he like it?'

'Mike, yes. He seems very adaptable. I'll talk to him tonight. I'll have to appeal to the Dawkins mentality.'

It took Maria a moment to click. Mike was Mike Dawkins. The Mike who had helped Maria learn her cycling years ago. The Mike that had accompanied her to Amsterdam on a ride that she still looked back on with pleasure.

'You okay Maria?'

'Yes. Sorry, I got a bit distracted there. I'm fine.'

'Great. Well, I'd better get going if I'm going to put this to him. But I think he'll like it.'

'I was just having another thought,' Maria said. 'Another possibility. Would you like another drink and I'll tell you about it.'

Actually, I wouldn't mind a coffee if that's alright,' Juliana said.

Maria made the coffee, chatting loudly from the kitchen about nothing in particular. In her mind she was having a slightly uncomfortable memory. The cycling had been a sort of intimate time but it had faded into history now. But now that moment when they had parted during that time came back to her. That moment when she had imagined his naked body pressed up to hers, of his strong, and hard, body … She shook her head to clear her thoughts.

She brought the coffees through and sat down. 'What I was going to add, and offer indeed, is another possibility. Spain. A lovely little apartment that you could have for a couple of weeks. Quite near the coast, a place called Calpe. You could have it quite cheaply too.'

Juliana's eyebrows lifted enough to show how surprised she was at this last minute thought. 'Go on,' was all she said.

'I own a flat in Spain that we go out to occasionally. And rent out at other times. When I say 'I' I mean Steve in fact. He owns the flat. We love it. It's really well positioned, well fitted out, and would make a good place.'

'Stephen owns it?'

'Yes. I'm not sure where he got it from. I think it was his parents and he was left it. More than one in fact. Anyway, it's his now.'

'And you could rent it out to Mike and I?'

'Well that was what I was thinking. It would also keep your costs down which I guess is never a bad thing.' Maria took some sheets out of her bag and handed one to Juliana.

Juliana took the sheet and browsed over it. 'Let me think about it tonight, and I'll get back to you. When do you need to know?'

'No hurry. It'll probably be a few weeks before we expect to start renting it for the coming year.'

'By the end of the week?'

'No problem.'

At home that night Juliana discussed the proposal over dinner. At first, she talked about her original plans in Italy and a few other suggestions she had had. Athens and other parts of Greece, and so on. Mike seemed excited particularly by Italy; he discussed it at length and it was clear that he was prepared to put his money into the plan.

But Juliana felt that she should mention the flat in Calpe, and told Mike about the offer. He liked the price and the idea of them spending some time together like a 'proper' couple, but in general he wasn't that keen. Calpe seemed like a cheap option, and he was keen to make a good impression on Juliana for this early stage in their relationship.

He thought through Italy more and more, and was pretty well decided on that. 'Let's go for Italy,' he said easily. 'It's got a lot going for it which will be good. We can do a few more things there.'

Juliana liked that he was prepared to think about economising.

'Okay,' she said. 'Italy it is. Which means we need to start working out where. Of all the places we talked about my money is on that bay.'

'Napoli.'

'Yup. Napoli. Somehow I can never get that name in my head. It sounds a great place. If we can find a hotel somewhere near the coast, we can do what that friend of yours, Sylvia was it, suggested and use the train line to get around. Let's go for it.'

'To be honest it's frankly likely to be better than Spain. I was only kind of interested in Calpe because of my friend Maria being there. I like that we're tying up together again; that feels good.' She laughed.

'She's your friend at the shop, isn't she? That's fair but we'd only be renting the place from her. That doesn't give you any time to develop anything with her. Your time together in the King's Road can do better.'

'Maria is a good person. I've known her for years, long before the shop, but she can be a bit 'random' at times.' Juliana smiled, 'I remember when we got some new dresses in we all liked them, there was almost no dislike in the shop, but then when the price came out she suddenly turned against them.'

'They were too dear?'

'No, too cheap. She thought it would bring the 'tone' of the place down and she rejected them.'

'Maybe she had a point.'

'I don't think so. She could have upped the price anyway. We do it all the time. But that's what I mean about her being a bit random; she can suddenly be a bit unpredictable. Anyway, we wouldn't only be renting from her. She's going to be out there too. She's staying at another of Stephen's places, somewhere nearby.'

Mike ate quietly for a short while. He seemed to be thinking that over, though Juliana couldn't see it made that much difference.

'I didn't realise that,' he said eventually. 'I guess you would get a chance to develop a closer time with her. Could be good.'

'Italy could be gooder,' she said with mischief on her face.

'But you talk about her a lot and I know you've wanted to be closer to her again, and it would be a good chance for me to meet her. Let's think about it.'

They chatted and chewed it over for a while, and eventually they decided that this year Calpe would be the place to be.

Juliana was delighted that he was bringing into the equation the fact that she wanted to recover her circle of friends, but instinctively felt on edge that he had changed his tune so easily.

Chelsea 2023

Mike saw the brochure on the sofa before he recognised it's meaning.

He was drifting around the place as he often did when he got back from a game of golf. It took him a while to get back into the throw of things after he had spent a few hours with friends plodding along the golf course. It had been a good game, the four of them on a well- developed course and all playing very well for the most part. He hadn't won, but he had done well, and probably slightly improved his handicap after he had handed in his score sheet. He was in a limbo that would take a half hour or so to leave him.

That time usually, as now, included making a cool cup of tea, looking at the Netflix programmes on TV, finding one that he might enjoy, and sitting down on the sofa and briefly looking at his news app that he had ignored all day. He had to push the brochure aside to sit down and he did so without acknowledgment.

Juliana arrived about an hour later, also as usual.

'Hi Mike.' Juliana kissed Mike on the cheek. 'How was your day?'

'Fine. Yours?'

'Do you know how often we ask each other that? In fact, not ask. It's not even a question. It's a chant. And do you know why it's a chant?'

Mike sat back and smiled. 'Tell me.'

'We're bored.' Juliana plonked down on the sofa with a bang that demanded attention. 'We have to do something about it.' She waited until he got his mouth open and at the exact moment added. 'Now.'

'Somehow I think you've got something in mind.' They smiled at each other.

Juliana went through to the kitchen, put on the kettle, and sorted out a few things from the fridge. She often started that way, but Mike came through and automatically started cutting and chopping and together they made a light tea.

'So, what have you got in mind?' he eventually asked.

'I'm not sure you're going to like it.'

He watched her, quietly. They had a good marriage so that didn't worry him. He didn't think there were any problems between them, nothing beyond the usual, anyway. But she did get some wacky ideas and he had learned to keep his head down.

She carried the meals through to the living room and he brought through some cutlery. In silent gestures he asked if they wanted to eat at the table, and she decided to eat on the sofa and watch some TV. They sat down, and he handed her the remote.

She put on the news, and they munched their food silently watching yet another set of diatribes about Brexit, Afghanistan, and how useless the American President was. Mike leaned over and picked up the remote, and muted the TV. He turned slightly in his seat to look directly at her.

'Come on. I've had a drink, a meal and I'm all out of the news. I can take it.' He laughed and she laughed with him.

Instead of replying she leaned over him, and picked up the brochure now laying on the arm.

'Calpe,' was all she said.

There wasn't much that could upset him, or distract him, but Calpe could. And he knew he had to tread carefully if he was to get beyond this.

'Calp,' was all he said.

'What?'

'Calp. That's what it's called nowadays. We knew it as Calpe when we went there donkeys' years ago, but nowadays they call it Calp. I think it was the original name, or the Spanish name, and now they're demanding it.'

'Well, I still like Calpe,' she insisted. With a smile.

'What about it?'

'I think we should go there. It would be great. We really enjoyed it there when we were there God-knows how many years ago.'

Tread carefully, he thought.

'There are a million other places in the world,' Mike offered. 'Why not find somewhere new and discover it for ourselves?'

'That isn't the point. I would like us to go back in time. To find it again. We found it as youngsters, as kids virtually. Let's go back and find it as adults.'

Mike thought this was already getting dodgy. Dodgier than he was ready to admit. But he was also thinking of the positive side. Maybe a week there, get it out of her system, and maybe they could move on. He was thinking already that if he could find a really, really good place to move on to after Calpe then he could erase it forever.

'Well, I guess that's an idea,' he offered, unenthusiastically. 'Maybe do a tour around. A few days in Calpe, and then drive on. Maybe take a couple of weeks to go through the Costa Blanca, or go inland. We've never done that before.'

He caught sight of her eyes for just a moment. She was keeping something from him. He suddenly felt very exposed. When she replied he knew for sure that it was a disguise.

'I was thinking…' she started. And stopped. 'I was thinking maybe we could take a month or two off work and make a real trip of it.'

That was possible, Mike thought. He knew that his own consultancy had just finished its major project, and that nothing important was on the horizon for a while. And he knew that Juliana was due a break; she had been saying so for a week or so. A month would give them time to 'do' Calpe, put it behind them, and have a very relaxing trip around Spain, maybe even around a wider stretch of Europe. He nodded, still not desperately enthusiastic.

She waved the brochure. 'I've been reading all about the place.'

'I doubt that it's changed much since we were there.'

'In fact, it has,' she replied quickly. 'Not much around the area south of the Penon where we were … in fact that's not even particularly true, there has been a lot of improvement there and so on … but north of the Penon is where it's all happened. What was just basically beaches and trees back in the 1980s is now as many skyscrapers and developments as in the southern section. It's become really huge. Big tourist place.' She waved the brochure at him again, confirming that she had been reading up on it all.

Mike realised that Juliana had been researching more than she was making out.

'Okay,' he said. 'We could fly into Alicante, hire a car and drive around the area for a week or so, visit Calpe, and maybe then fly south and see Gibraltar and Malaga. Which I think is the Costa del Sol. Would be slightly warmer down there too.'

Juliana shook her head firmly. Too firmly, thought Mike. He raised an eyebrow; no other part of him had the courage to move at the moment.

'No. I want to really get to know the place. I thought we could hire a flat or a villa for the month, maybe two months, and live there like real Spanish people. Get to really know the place. Maybe pick up a bit of the language.'

'Calpe?' was all Mike replied.

'Yes. We've never done anything like that before.'

Mike felt a serious sweat breaking out under his clothes. He hoped, desperately, that he wasn't visibly sweating where Juliana could see him. This was a nightmare. He had thought he might be able to hijack the plan but Juliana seemed determined, and Mike couldn't see a way out. No. No. No. He kept saying that silently to himself.

'Why 'no'?' she asked.

Alright. Not so silently obviously. 'I just meant…' He stumbled. He tried to get his thinking in order, he didn't want to babble. Mainly, he still didn't want to put his foot in his mouth even if that would have shut him up. 'I just meant that Calpe is a small place. Very touristy. Fun to be around for a while but not a place to spend real time.'

She said nothing. Just waiting.

He went on in the quiet. 'I think what you're suggesting is a great idea. But there are some wonderful places we could spend a month or so. Maybe inland would be a better place to explore. Cordoba. Cartagena. Madrid itself. Calpe is too small.'

She still said nothing. But he could see in her eyes a coldness and a darkness that was frightening him. He knew – knew! – that her desire to visit Calpe was not an innocent one.

Calpe 1984

The one thing that Mike wanted was to make this holiday a successful one for the two of them. He sensed that Juliana had some suspicions about his choice, and it was making it tough from the start.

After multiple delays, the plane landed at Alicante at almost midnight – several hours late - and there had then been even more waiting while they found someone to hand over the car they had hired.

'I booked it weeks ago. They can't have a problem getting it ready.'

'Someone once told me that the most important word in Spain is 'ish,' Juliana said. 'The banks open at nine- ish, the bars close at eleven-ish. And I think our car will be ready immediately-ish.' Mike noticed that Juliana was at least in a light mood.

'Great'.

That turned out to be right. The paperwork was all there, the car was ready and everything was arranged. But it took over half an hour to do what should have taken minutes. And after a delayed flight, and a long day, it was just one more annoyance. The mistake that Mike made was to make light of it; Juliana had been easy to that point but his humour irritated her.

'Let's just get out of here. I need bed.'

Another issue was that the car was not the one ordered and no one could tell them why their medium sized car was now a small three door one. They gave up trying to find someone who could explain what had happened or better still change it, and they grudgingly accepted the car.

They eventually drove off towards Calpe.

It turned out to be a three-quarter hour drive, possibly faster than usual as there was very little traffic around at that time of night. One spot where they slowed down was about halfway, and there the traffic was heavy and the lights many; they had passed Benidorm. That was a place they were keen to avoid; noisy, lively and mostly full of Brits they didn't want to meet.

At around half one in the morning they drove into Calpe.

'Where is this place? Mike asked.

'It's called Vista Maritima.'

'I couldn't care less. Where is it?' The drive had worn Mike out. Knowing the Spanish were hot on drunk drivers and being fairly certain he had overdone it he had been nervous. Now he was nervous, irritable and lost. 'It just says C Gibraltar on these sheets you got Jooles.'

Juliana looked over at them again. 'That's what Maria said. She seemed to indicate it was obvious.'

'Maybe more obvious in the daylight and when everyone isn't falling asleep.'

It turned out that C indicated 'street' so it was just Gibraltar Street, or something like that. They slowed down a couple of times and an impatient Juliana asked out of the window if anyone knew Gibraltar Street. No one seemed to understand them but one person made a lot of left turn gestures which they followed. They turned into a road, never seeing a name anywhere, and stopped to try and get some better idea of where they were.

'What's this place called we're heading for?' Mike asked.

'Vista Maritima,' Juliana called back.

Mike pointed. 'Like that?'

Juliana followed where his finger was pointing. It turned out they were parked outside a tall apartment block called exactly that.

'If that's it, it's more by luck than judgement.'

It was it, and they parked the car underneath as Maria had told them, and took the lift to the ninth floor. They opened the apartment door, threw their suitcases into a pile in the living room, and thought of bed. But they calmed down after the drive with a coffee, and a quick look around the place, which seemed very good, agreed which bedroom to commandeer, and went to bed.

The morning started peacefully. Mike and Juliana got up together, and they looked over the kitchen getting the hang of it, checking out what they had. The apartment was very good. They had an 'end' apartment which meant that they had a balcony at both the front and back of the block. Both bedrooms looked out of the back balcony and the living room looked out of the front one. The two bedrooms were good sized and comfortable, and the living room and kitchen were linked and had plenty of space. As there was only the two of them they felt the extra space gave them room, and a sense of freedom.

Soon they had tidied up a lot of the stuff they had scattered around last night, and having found a 'welcome' pack of breakfast food in the fridge they had prepared omelettes and cereal to start the day with.

'We'll need to get some food in,' was Juliana main contribution of the morning.

Mike thought that perhaps the night had been forgotten and they could get on with their holiday. Juliana seemed to agree.

London 2023

'We've got the last of the students to pass through the training,' Audrey said, looking through the papers in her hand. 'but that's all booked. We have them in three batches over the next three weeks.'

Audrey's desk was hardly organised, though that is exactly what she claimed it was. She put her notes on the table and they instantly disappeared into it. Mike looked away, knowing that he could hardly face such disorganisation but also knowing that somehow Audrey could, and would immediately find what she needed to when it was necessary.

Mike nodded. 'What about the implementation of the last changes?'

'Carl said they were all underway. They've been planned over a few months, but I think you're away from all that if I understand correctly.' Audrey whipped out a file from somewhere to prove it.

Mike slapped shut the folder he had been holding. 'What else have we got coming up?' He looked over the few sheets and files on the desk that he could recognise. 'We've got the Carson project. But the training is only just starting for that, and my involvement won't start for several months. The Harvey project: do I have anything outstanding on that?'

'No,' Audrey confirmed. 'Richard and Oscar are opening all that up, but I don't think you'll have anything to do for some time.' She picked up another folder from the desk. 'We also have a pretty full compliment working while you're away. I think the only person booked to be away is Purdey. She's been humming and harring about a holiday but she booked it just a day or so ago.'

'Purdey?' Mike thought a while. 'Is she the new girl?'

Audrey put down the files she had been holding. 'Yes, she is. Been here a couple of months. Have you worked with her yet?'

'No.'

'Well the people I've spoken to who she has worked with say she's very good, and very likeable. But I must admit I do have some doubts about her. She's … I don't know … a bit sparky. Or flaky. I don't know how to describe it. She's really friendly and helpful, and then she can just lose it in an instant. Really get snappy. And it doesn't seem to matter who she's with, senior people get it in the neck too.'

'Should we get rid of her?'

Audrey thought a moment, but shook her head. 'She always gets over it, equally quickly, and is very apologetic. People say they appreciate that, and they all tell me she is a hard worker. No, I don't think you should get rid of her, but I just have a … strange … feeling about her sometimes.'

'Is her being absent a problem?'

'No. She would be working with either Richard or Oscar but they confirmed they can manage.'

Mike dismissed it. He had enough to think about, and worry about, not to care that much about a new girl trying to find her place in the company. 'Fine. I feel a bit nervous being away from the office for a month I must admit,' Mike said, taking his chance. 'In fact, if I'm needed here I'd prefer to be here. I don't want to let anyone down.'

'Not at all Mike. This is the perfect time for you. You've got a gap and you should use it. Your wife must be really looking forward to it.'

'She is. But I'm guessing that she might have trouble sorting it out. I did suggest to her that we should maybe hold back for a few months and arrange it later.'

'What did she say?'

'Didn't want to. She seemed very keen.'

'That's it then,' Audrey said. 'She's ready. You're lined up for it. It should be great. Do it and have an exciting time.'

'I suppose …. '

Audrey sat back, simultaneously throwing the notes she had into the black hole that was open in front of them both. 'If we do need you the world is a smaller place than it used to be. We can call you, or email you. You can be back in contact with us in minutes. You were saying the other day that you could run your office from the top of a mountain or the middle of a desert so long as you had wi-fi. Now's the time to prove it; not that Spain is a desert.'

Mike gave up, and just nodded.

'Where are you off to anyway?'

'Calpe.'

'Calpe? Never heard of it. Whereabouts is that? One of the islands?'

'No, it's on the mainland. On the Costa Blanca.'

'Sounds like a new place for you. I hope it works out well.'

'I've been there before. In fact, we both have. But a long time ago.'

'You and Juliana have been there?'

'Yes.'

'I'm stunned. I can hardly believe it.'

Mike looked at her uncertainly. 'Why? It's quite a tourist place I think; maybe more so than it used to be. And it's near Benidorm which is very well known.'

Audrey laughed. 'You've never mentioned being there before.'

Mike shrugged, but the humorous look on Audrey's face goaded him on. 'There is something you're hiding from me and I'm not getting it.'

Audrey shook her head. 'Nothing. Really.'

'No. Go on.'

Audrey knew him well enough to share private comments so she dived in. 'You're an open person,' she started. 'And everyone says they know everywhere in the world you've been.' She laughed again.

'I'm still not catching up.'

'You talk about your holidays. In fact, to be truthful you speak about everything. It's a positive thing, believe me. It's something you're well known for. You go on holiday, and you come back and tell us all about it.'

Mike was beginning to get it. 'You mean I bore everyone to tears?'

'No.' Audrey held her hands out. 'No, really. You make these things sound really interesting. And you go to some incredible places. After you came back from Japan I was really taken with your descriptions of the parks and the shrines. And the monuments. And your description of Mount Fuji. You might remember that I went to Japan two years later because you just led me out there. And I loved it. What you might not know is that three other people also holidayed in Japan after that; you really made an impact.'

'Sounds like I should have got commission?'

'Absolutely. But it's really lovely to hear. Genuinely. And the same when you went to Cuba. And to Mexico. You just bring these places alive.'

Mike smiled and nodded, and started to walk away.

'But,' Audrey persisted. 'you've never mentioned Calpe. Not once I think.'

Mike thought about that and realised immediately what it meant. He tried very hard to keep the smile on his face but he could feel it fading fast. 'It was a very long time ago. Too long for remembrances.'

'When did you go to Formentera?'

'Formentera?' Mike was starting to get irritated with Audrey's persistence. 'That was even further back. I was a kid, virtually.'

'Exactly. That's how I remembered it. But I feel I know all about Formentera, though in fact I've forgotten where it is. But you told us all about it once. I would put money on it that you've never been anywhere you haven't told us about.'

Mike nodded slightly.

'Apart from Calpe.'

Mike was now trying harder still to keep the smile on his face, but it was fading fast.

Audrey got in first. 'So why is that? Do you have a naughty secret about Calpe?'

Mike could sense the innocent mischief in her voice. And he wanted, very much, to join in with it but also to get this conversation over quickly. He did not want to labour on about Calpe longer than he had to. 'None at all. Just a place that wasn't that much to talk about I guess.'

Audrey folded her arms and looked straight at him, grin on her face. 'I think there's a naughty secret out there. I'm thinking suntanned blonde to start with.'

'Afraid not. But I'll look out for one when I'm there.'

Something he said clicked with Audrey. She said nothing, but she started to back away from the conversation. She could not put her finger on it, but she could feel there really was something she had stumbled on. And she felt it was a door she wished she hadn't opened. She folded up her notes and tucked them under her arm.

'Well, I hope it all works out well for you,' she said. 'I'd better be getting along.'

Mike was pleased to move on. 'Busy day?'

'Busy for the next few hours anyway. I've got a meeting with Oscar in about a half hour and I need to bone up on it.' She walked away, and closed the door behind her.

Mike looked out of the window for a while, not seeing London but looking down, from a considerable height, on Calpe. After a while he sat down heavily in a chair and stayed there for a while.

Calpe was filling his thinking.

Calpe 1984

The first days were typical holiday, and basic. They bought some food for breakfast but decided they would probably eat out for dinner. Lunch was possible, but uncertain. What they did discover is that they could buy booze downstairs that was a little questionable. You took your empty 2 litre plastic bottle of cola down to the store downstairs and you could buy 2 litres of brandy, or Tia Maria, or other drinks, for about fifty pence. Heaven knows how they produced that, and they did worry a little as to what chemicals were in the drink, but they tasted good. One night they drank through a whole bottle of Tia Maria while playing cards; that seemed such a promising idea they bought another bottle for the next night. They played cards, and kept offering each other the drink but neither took it. In fact, they never touched it at all, and Mike found he was unable to drink Tia Maria again for about six months. 'The bottle we bought is probably still lying about somewhere', Juliana suggested much later.

The days were hot, sunny and peaceful, and they walked about the town and spent a couple of days just sitting having coffees or drinks or ice creams and looking out to sea, looking at the leather and silver ornaments that groups of street vendors laid out on the beaches, and generally getting suntanned or drunk or both.

In a short time they would be splitting up and spending a few days apart. Juliana had suggested that they should do some things separately; she was very keen they should grow together but also that they maintain their own space. She had some friends back in Alicante she was going to spend two or three days with. She discussed with Mike what he planned to do. 'I'm going to do some touring, probably just around this area,' he said. 'Maybe go inland a bit. I'll be away from a regular phone but I have your number, where you'll be, so I'll keep in touch.'

One thing they spent time enjoying was the view of a huge rock called the Penon de Ifach which rises a thousand feet on the coast, dominating the town. Both locals and visitors either climb up it or watch others climb up it. Mike planned to climb up it; Juliana held back from commitment.

The atmosphere changed when Maria arrived. She had been staying in Les Bassetes nearby, apparently in another apartment Stephen owned.

'Good morning guys,' she said to them both.

'Morning Maria.' Juliana brought her into the flat and pointed her to a comfortable sofa. Perhaps he was 'on edge' but Mike felt a chill descend over the room.

'Good morning Maria,' Mike said. He kept his voice light, tried to smooth over any issues. He hoped that perhaps Juliana didn't know that he and Maria knew each other, or knew each other that much. Her next comment, 'It's been a long time Mike. Good to see you,' put paid to that.

Mike was having trouble identifying his concerns. Was he afraid that Juliana would imagine something between them? Was there anything between them? Nothing had happened certainly, but would it have if circumstances had been different?

Whatever he wondered, Maria seemed to go for the throat. 'Mike and I were together in Amsterdam a few years back when I did that ride. I probably told you about that Juliana.'

'Mike mentioned it a long time ago. He trained you, in fact, didn't he?'

'He did indeed. And supported me all through the ride, which was a few days.'

Mike chipped in, looking for some control. 'There were about forty of us there,' he said. 'And we all supported each other.'

'To say nothing of introducing me to the world of drugs,' said Maria. Mike could cheerfully have killed her; it seemed clear to him that she was stirring it up for them.

'Now that he didn't tell me,' Juliana said, smiling.

'It was nothing like that,' Mike said. 'Smoking pot is legal in Amsterdam and we went to a place where we could buy some, lots of other cycle riders from our team were there too, and we had a couple of spliffs. It was a nothing. Maria, you're over-dressing it.' He laughed to show how 'nothing' it was.

Maria laughed, hard and loud, and Mike did his best to try it too. Juliana came over next to them, smiling with a stare. 'You two enjoying yourself?'

Maria broke the moment. 'I just popped in to see you were all settled and okay. The flat what you hoped for?

They both nodded, and Juliana said how good it was and that they expected to have a great time. Maria seemed happy by that and walked towards the door to leave.

'Oh, I meant to show you the switches in case you get a power-out,' Maria called back to Juliana. 'It's over here.' Maria led Juliana over to the kitchen and showed her the white box of switches. 'If you get a power out most of the time you can just turn it all back on by throwing whichever switch turns off. They're all marked; up is on and down is off.' She left Juliana looking at the box. 'I'll see you later.'

Maria walked back towards the door, checked that Juliana was still looking in the box, and diverted briefly towards Mike on her way back to the front door. 'Call me sometime' was all she said, quietly.

And Mike had no doubts about her intentions.

Chelsea 2023

Mike got home early that evening. He knew that Juliana would not get home until later, he needed time to think through the problems that re-visiting Calpe could produce.

But could it actually produce any? That was the paradox. He felt so frightened by the idea of revisiting Calpe, but he could think of almost nothing that could happen that should trouble him. He had spent a long time; virtually all of his adult life, worrying about Calpe and its history with him, yet it was over thirty-five years ago and he was safe to assume that nothing could arise now.

So, was he just worrying now because he always did? Or was there something that he had only recognised subconsciously and could not yet frame a picture of? It was an unsettling thought. But he had hardly thought consciously about Calpe for decades; in fact, it was only Juliana's desire to go back there that had triggered his current fears.

But that was another fact in the equation. Why did Juliana want to go back there? She had never mentioned the place in the past thirty-odd years? So why now? What had triggered her desire to go back there.

Sometimes he could see a bright sunny landscape. Maybe she just wished to return to revisit her memories and perhaps enjoy and even enhance them. And sometimes he could see a dark and brooding vista, shrouded in shadows and obscure movements, with things moving in cloudy silhouettes. Sometimes Juliana was just another thing of beauty in the sweet, perfumed, panorama. And sometimes she was the phantom haunting the spectre in the dark; hunting …. What? Hunting him?

He browsed Calpe on his mobile; flicking through the online outlines and brochures about the town and the surroundings. He flicked through it, but there was nothing unexpected about it. It mainly advertised the beaches and the hotels, and it set out the places to visit. It had a history of the town including its life as a fishing village, and its longer history, back over three thousand years, and coming forward through the Romans to the times of the Christians and Muslims living there in harmony and troubled only by pirate attacks from time to time.

Popularity of the fish market, and the fish restaurants of which the town had a plethora. It highlighted the Rock, the Penon de Ifach, which was hardly surprising as it was the major feature on virtually any view from the town and the most popular tourist attraction, climbed by many tens of thousands every year.

The Penon, of course, was the centre of Mike's concerns. Juliana was aware of that part of the history of their visit, but, Mike was sure, not at all aware of his role in it.

He looked at papers on the table where Juliana kept random items. There were some notes in Juliana's handwriting. Mike didn't want to spy on her, but he also knew he couldn't avoid it. He read the notes he could without moving anything; but they were innocuous. Possible dates, plane options, some notes that looked like probably names of villas or apartments but none that he recognised and therefore none that should bother him.

He scattered the top notes aside and read through the ones beneath them. Eventually he picked them all up and read through them, dropping them back on the table as carefully as he could remember. But they were pointless notes; possible food to eat, drinks to buy, notes of a few restaurants they had eaten in thirty-odd years ago and many of which, he was sure, would now be long gone.

Eventually he threw them all down and sat back. He was coming to the satisfactory conclusion that Juliana was just looking for a chance to wander through their memories. He calmed down.

He poured himself a scotch and ice, and walked through to the kitchen to see if he could find a snack. His mind was still concerned about Juliana's motives, but he was feeling easier about it and thinking more and more about crisps or a sandwich or some fruit as he mooched around.

It was while he was stripping a banana, and still standing next to the fruit bowl, that he saw the stack of bills and other papers stacked up behind it, using it as a bookend or letter rack. He picked them up more to dismiss them than investigate them. They were a couple of bills, and a petrol receipt, and some advertising papers on electric cars and some more on solar panels. Juliana must be thinking ecologically.

But in amongst them was a sheet of paper. He looked at it and saw immediately that it was a print of an email Juliana, presumably, had received.

"Thank you for talking to me this morning. It was a great relief. The mystery that has worried me for years is still a mystery, but at least

I have you to help share it with me. If we can get together as we discussed that would be very comforting, Perhaps I could call you again soon? Many thanks, Phil."

Mike looked at it a while, and thought of the people he knew that Juliana knew, but he could not think of a 'Phil'. Whoever he was, Mike had no knowledge of him.

It told him very little, except that it put him very much on edge. What had started to look like an innocent thought out of the sunny landscape was now definitely looking like a shadow in the dark edges.

Calpe 1984

Mike parked the car and looked, yet again, at the wall of the Playa Hotel. He had telephoned Maria as she had suggested, Maybe (definitely) he was just walking into a situation that he should avoid, but he was confident that he could walk away from it if necessary.

Mike got out of the car and locked the doors. He circled around with his eyes and walked towards the hotel, positioned towards the beach. Before he got there, he saw Maria walking towards him. He could feel the tingling in different parts of his body, some of which he had hardly felt since he was a teenager.

Maria was stunningly attractive; smooth skin, longish jet-black straight hair, owl-like sunglasses that somehow seemed to accentuate her features rather than hide them. And a very engaging smile. They greeted each other.

'Come in,' Maria said and led him into the building. 'Drink?'

Mike nodded, and allowed her to take his hand as they walked in. He was lying to himself; he knew that now. His old attractions from years ago were weakening his resolve. He reasoned he had fancied a lot of women in the past and nothing had happened, but this time he knew he might be pushing himself too far.

Juliana was away for some days, which they had planned before they came out here. She had suggested that they have a few days apart which would be refreshing for them both. Juliana and Mike had agreed that they should both get used to alone-time from each other. Neither of them wanted to feel that they lived in each other's pockets, or couldn't exist easily without the other. At first Mike thought it a slightly strange idea, but then he agreed to it, as if it was a good idea, because he could see that it would give him a chance to follow up on a few things, It didn't occur to him that her suggestion would give her the exact same chances, and that she intended to take them.

So, when Maria had made the offer Mike had decided to accept it. Somewhere in his head he knew he was daring himself to accept, or resist, the chances. But in fact he was, more honestly, just waiting to see which way the wind blew.

Maria put down her drink and sat up. 'I have a suggestion I am hoping you would be agreeable to.'

'Go on.'

'It's a bit of a reminiscence.' She was teasing him, perhaps goading him.

'Go on.'

'Outside the building, round by the car park, there are two bikes. I hired them for us both. I was hoping we could cycle around. Probably around Calpe. Perhaps a little further. Do you fancy it?'

That had come out of the blue. He had been going over the possibilities, particularly since she had invited him to a hotel. But he suddenly felt very relieved and genuinely pleased that her suggestion was so innocuous. 'I fancy that a lot.'

She smiled.

'Let's hope I'm still as fit as I used to be.'

She smiled even more broadly. 'I always thought you were,' she said.

They walked outside, and Maria showed him the bikes. They were strong, adaptable bikes that should take care of any hills they were likely to find around them.

'What about clothes? I haven't got any with me.'

'Neither have I. We're both wearing shorts. T shirts. This won't be the Tour de France. Or the Tour de Spain anyway. We'll be fine.'

Mike nodded.

Maria flicked her legs over the cycle frame and checked the brakes and steering. She watched Mike do the same.

'This wouldn't upset Juliana would it?' she asked. 'I'm not sure if she's a cyclist.'

'No, she wouldn't mind this.'

Maria leaned over and stroked his arm. 'Good,' she said. And they cycled off away from the beach-side of the hotel.

They cycled for a few hours, with a couple of stops for ice creams and drinks. Maria took a couple of opportunities to close up to Mike, and once gave him a peck on the cheek when she handed him an ice cream. Just before plonking a chunk on his nose and running back laughing. They took it easy, and climbed any hills they had to deal with, maybe just so that they could shout loudly with joy as they freewheeled down. They circled Calpe, and cycled in both the north and south sections of the roads around the Penon de Ifach. Then they left the circular route and cycled north of Calpe up the coast roads. It was a beautiful day, hot but not too hot, bright and sunny. They cycled for half an hour or so until Maria stopped ahead of Mike, and got off the bike.

'Where are we?' Mike asked.

'Moraira.'

Mike got off and looked around. It was a fairly typical coastal town, decent beach and a fair few old buildings to ponder.

'It's a lovely place. Come and see a little more of it.' Maria didn't wait to be answered, just cycled away again and Mike had to follow. They cycled away from the shore and into what seemed to be more rural areas. Eventually she drove into the gates of complex of very old-style looking villas. He followed her in and jumped off the bike next to her.

The frontage was extraordinary. It looked only like a set of cemetery gates could look. Man picks girl up, man takes girl home, home is a cemetery, she turns to him, and bares her fangs ... Mike smiled, but actually shook his head to clear the strange thought from his mind.

'What is special about this place?'

'I live here.'

'You live in there?' Oh dear, that wasn't very tactfully put, he thought.

'That's where the apartment is. Inside.'

'What is this place?'

'There's a sign on the wall. It'll tell you.' She pointed, smiling. 'Can you see it?'

Mike followed her to the front entrance gates where she pointed out the inscription. Apparently, the place had been built years ago by somebody to house their estate workers. Inside the 'cemetery gates' were in fact fourteen beautiful houses, now subdivided into many flats.

'The first ever housing estate I should think.' Maria said. 'Locally anyway. And you thought you had invented them in England I'll bet.'

Maria pointed through the gates and several trees to a clump of lights burning indistinctly in the distance. 'That's our apartment. Through there.'

Mike nodded. He knew he was being thrown a lead. And one he should cycle away from right now.

The night was cloudless and very, very hot and muggy. The moon was nearly full. No traffic sounds at all - they could have been in the heart of the country. It was so still and quiet that behind them they could even hear the 'clicking' crepitations of the bikes cooling down.

'This may sound silly but I get a little afraid of the walk from here to the apartment, late at night. Would it trouble you very much if I asked you to walk with me?' Maria sidled up close to him. He thought immediately that Maria would not get afraid if ghosts and goblins charged out en-masse; she'd probably put them all in their place in one move. But he felt unable to resist the lead he was being offered. He thought not of Maria, but of Juliana, and their easy life together. But when he looked at Maria's smiling face again he dismissed Juliana from his mind and realised he was lost if Maria pursued this.

'Not at all.'

'You don't get afraid?' she asked.

'No.' This from the man with vampires from Hammer horror movies in his mind just at seeing a pair of rusty old gates!

They walked through the gates, pushed them shut behind them. Steamy hot and quiet, the two of them crunched slowly down the gravel drive. Maria took his arm with both hands.

'I'm sorry,' she said. 'I suffer from night-blindness. Do you mind?'

'I don't mind at all. But if you hold me like this all the way you may have to fight me off at the other end.'

'I'm not likely to fight you off now I've got you here, am I?'

Mike took her hands off his arm and re-arranged things a bit more comfortably. Sensuously. He was very aware of the smells of her perfume and her body. He was conflicted between knowing he should stop this before it got out of hand, and feeling drawn in where he knew he wanted to be.

'If you haven't seen these houses you'll love them. Oak beams and plaster walls. And you know those - what do you call them? - gargoyles?'

'Gargoyles. Yes, I think so. Pretty weird in Spain I would think.'

'Well, they have them inside the villa as well as outside. We have them on the ceiling in our kitchen. It's not as strange as it might seem though; people think of Spain, and this area, as modern and high rise, but there's a lot of history here.' They stopped outside the villa and turned to face each other, still holding hands.

'Coffee?' she asked.

There was mischief even in the question. Mike turned towards her and nodded, and she leaned in and kissed him. It was a friendly kiss, nothing passionate. But as he slightly backed away she moved closer and kissed him hard and passionately. He knew he was at the turning point, and he knew he should turn away now. He leaned forward and kissed her. It really was a natural response. Something about that kiss felt like the best kiss he'd ever had in his life. Not overly sexual, not overly erotic, though tinged with both. It was incredibly gentle and long. Full of sensuality and the heat of the night to come.

Mike felt how he was being drawn in, and he thought back to their time in Amsterdam. He had fancied her then but she had not been available. Perhaps she had fancied him though she had been clear that she was sticking with her boyfriend. He doubted that was changing; he thought that perhaps this was just a diversion. It made him feel better if it was.

Maria showed him around the apartment while the coffee bubbled. There was an awkward moment when Maria pointed at a closed bedroom door.

With no preamble Maria turned and held both Mike's arms. He lifted his hands around her waist, pulled her close, kissed. This kiss was different, very sexual. Probing tongues and gentle teeth. Her hands were enjoying the feel of his backside as she pulled him closer still. They explored each other's bodies and mouths, mutually coming apart slowly.

'I'm going to have a shower. I'm too hot and sticky. Will you join me?'

There was just a twinge of disappointment when 'the chase' ended and all the cards were on the table. Particularly since Mike had never quite managed to get the initiative. But some new energy took over; he felt it as she spoke.

'I happen to be the best back-soaper in the country,' he said.

'Lucky I found you.'

The shower was a small, odd-shaped cubicle built under an expansive staircase. They both went in. Maria leaned over and started the shower. Mike slipped off his t-shirt and threw it in the corner by the door. Maria, more sensibly, closed the lid of the toilet, slipped off her shirt, and laid it on that. Mike continued throwing his clothes onto his pile.

Maria's figure lived up to the promise. Astonishingly slim waist, coffee-cream coloured skin, large breasts. In the shower, Maria reached for shower gel and poured gallons of it all over them both. It made them slippery as eels and heightened the tactile sensations. Eyes closed, Mike took in the feelings. Really, really electric feelings charged through every muscle. For a bit they tried soaping each other but that's not as easy as it sounds. They kept knocking each other off balance. They went back to sliding their hands over each other.

Mike expected to get worked up there and then flop down in the huge bed he'd seen earlier. Maria had other plans and wanted sex there and then. Mike turned off the shower and they got out of the confined little cubicle into the room which wasn't much bigger; and scattered both sets of clothes over the floor. Mike knelt and pulled Maria down next to him.

They laid down; kissing and touching and stroking and licking. They were talking to each other too, but with no idea what they were saying. Something about the evening or the car, but they were just noises really. Mike spent a while banging his head against the toilet and getting his toes caught in the shower curtain, but it all passed almost unnoticed.

They weren't very harmonised at first; Mike was trying to keep it going as long as possible but Maria virtually pulled him inside her and squeezed and squeezed an orgasm out of him. She was so incredibly hot inside that Mike got quickly excited and came almost immediately.

They slipped back and spent a while stroking and cuddling and then they started again. Mike didn't last much longer that time either; Maria had a way of tonguing his ear that went from head to toe. When Mike cupped her nipples in his mouth and flicked them with his tongue her reaction would have made a monk give up the habit. Then they crashed back again for a rest, physically apart so that they could cool down. The stone floor was delightful on their backs, their clothes now scrunched up in the corners of the room.

Mike laid there listening to her breathing.

And thinking about Juliana.

He fancied Maria and obviously she fancied him. But now that it was over his feeling for Juliana hit him like a sledgehammer. He loved her. As he thought through the two situations he couldn't reconcile them. And he really couldn't work out where he was lying to Juliana, and where he was lying to himself.

When Maria got up and walked through to the bedroom Mike was glad to follow just to give himself something else to think of. Maria laid on the bed. Mike wandered around the room looking at the books and papers on her desk and scattered over the chairs, restless, needing to work off excess energy (strangely enough!)

He was naked, and felt easy about it. He had a good figure, and was quite proud of his physique. He postured, laughing, and she laughed too at his exaggerated pose.

'Stay there,' she suddenly shouted. 'Stay right there.'

He started to turn slightly, but she shouted again. 'No, stay exactly as you are.'

Mike froze, with a puzzled expression on his face. Maria went quickly across the room, picked up her polaroid camera and brought it back to where she had been standing. She waved it towards him. 'Do you mind if I take a photo. I promise you, you'll love this.'

Mike didn't feel that relaxed about her taking a picture, but also this seemed to be a bad time to say no. He tried to get the puzzled expression off his face, and at the same time he shrugged and smiled. 'Go ahead.'

Maria moved slightly, told him to stay very still, and then she lined up the picture and took a photo.

'Okay,' she said. 'Relax. It's done.'

Mike sat back, but the puzzled look on his face returned. 'So, what was that all about.'

'Maria was flapping the polaroid sheet about. 'You're going to love this,' she said. Then she handed him the picture for him to see.

They both laughed out loud, and very soon it broke into the kind of uncontrolled laughter that happens once in a blue moon.

'I had to catch you quickly,' she explained. On the photo was a picture of the naked Mike, facing her with an innocence on his face. But behind him was a statue of an angel with huge wings. Mike was between the picture and Maria and the picture she had taken was Mike blocking out the angel so that it appeared – very accurately – like he had the huge wings coming out of his back. What's more the wings and his skin were very similar in colour. It really looked like Mike had the wings growing out of him, and it was so funny the two of them laughed for a while. For the rest of the night, in fact, one or both of them would just erupt into laughter spontaneously. Even after it had become 'not so funny anymore' they couldn't stop laughing now and again.

'Don't forget to destroy that,' Mike reminded her.

'But you look like such a beautiful angel,' she said.

'Yes. Not counting my cock pointing out at you.'

'I didn't know you would be embarrassed.'

Mike turned up the corner of his mouth.

'I know, I know,' said Maria. 'It's not the sort of picture I want found, I'll get rid of it.'

Mike went back to the bed, and laid down.

Both of them laid back on the bed, and they felt more relaxed and a little 'closer'. Chatting turned to cuddling, cuddling to kissing and the kissing got stronger and more vigorous,

Quietly laying there, looking at the ceiling – and one of those weird gargoyle-like things – Mike started thinking.

He could feel regret rising to the surface. Not happiness. Not ecstasy. Not even conquest. Regret? Regret because he knew he'd just had the best sex of his life, with a stunning woman, in just the right circumstances and he knew it wasn't going to be repeated. Even if they did it again nothing would be like that first time. He was wishing that it had happened in Amsterdam, a time when there would have been no regrets or guilt. Now he had Juliana to think about, and it complicated everything.

They had sex just once more that night, but it was almost a friendly gesture, with little passion. A gentle, quiet, un-athletic tussle that was so clearly going to be their way of saying 'goodbye and thank you.' Or so he thought.

They dressed and chatted lightly, had a light drink, and joked. And then Maria said something that stopped him dead in his tracks.

Spain 2023

'We are at thirty-five thousand feet and descending. We should be in Alicante airport within the next thirty minutes,' the Captain was saying. 'Weather is very good. Sunshine expected for at least the next week. No clouds. No winds. And a temperature of thirty-one degrees, as it has been for the past twenty thousand years.'

There was a polite round of laughter through the aircraft. Mike looked at Juliana and smiled. She was packing up her tablet, disconnecting the earphones, and tidying up her backpack. Mike stuffed the magazine he had been reading into the back of the chair in front of him, and sat back.

He watched out of the windows as the fields and buildings on the right, and the sea to the left, got closer as the plane dropped. He saw, with a troubling sense of discomfort, the Penon de Ifach jutting out into the sea and passing behind him as the plane descended. He had been looking out for it, as if by seeing it he would put the feelings it produced behind him. But he landed with the same sense of disquiet.

'It feels good to be back,' Juliana said as they walked down the plane steps in the heat.

'Yes, it does,' Mike said automatically. But thinking the opposite.

They walked into the building, and queued for a brief time to display their passports and then pass through to where they would collect their hire-car. Juliana had done most of the booking and Mike stayed behind her as she went to the counter and laid her documents out on the counter. She called him over once so that they could take a copy of his driving licence, and then he dropped back again to let her finish. Shortly afterwards they walked through the building, as directed, to the car park where they picked up a mid-range Peugeot.

'Do you know that in Spain you can be fined for washing your car in the street?' Juliana smiled at Mike.

'No,' he replied. 'Why did you look that up?'

'I didn't. I just found it while I was looking up more relevant things. I also found out that you can be fined if you drive bare-chested, barefooted, or wearing flip flops.'

'Can women be fined driving bare chested?' Mike laughed.

'Yes. I also found out that in France you have to carry your own breathalyser.'

'We're not in France.'

'I looked up lots of rules. Do you know that we have to drive on the right over here?'

They both laughed at their joint sarcasm. 'Now I think I had read that somewhere. In most, or all, of Europe in fact.'

'All except Italy.'

Mike stopped and faced her directly. 'They don't drive on the right in Italy?' he asked, seriously.

'They might,' she replied. 'But no-one's ever been able to find out for sure.' They both laughed their way to their car.

Juliana drove; it took around an hour to reach Calpe. The biggest delay was getting out of Alicante airport, and there was some delay as they passed Benidorm, but about an hour later they drove into the town, with Mike looking at the map.

Juliana had hired a villa on the Avenue Felip VI; and it took no time to drive to it. They parked towards the back of the villa, got out and walked around before unloading the car.

Mike had to admit it was a good villa; and a good deal more spacious than the apartment they had stayed in almost forty years ago. It could sleep six, though there were only the two of them. It had a good, private pool of some reasonable size, a beautiful dining table outside next to a spectacular bar-b-que, a spacious and well-laid out kitchen that led straight out to the pool and bar-b-que. It had a dining room with a generous granite table and elaborately carved chairs that led directly to the lounge which had a TV many cinemas would have been proud of. Three double bedrooms were each equipped with very well laid out bathrooms, each containing a bath, shower, toilet and bidet. Each bedroom was differently decorated; one very modern, one very old-styled, and one plain and simple.

They spent the rest of the day unpacking and spreading themselves out through the villa. They found a table tennis table laid out for play in the garden and they had a few games while laughing and chatting about the weeks to come.

'This is a beautiful villa,' Mike said, in genuine praise of Juliana's choice.

'Thank you. This is going to be a good holiday.'

At that point he knocked the ball off the table and it bounced across the tiles and into the swimming pool. They chased each other round the pool trying to fish it out, and in the end Juliana hooked it in with a lawn rake. They finished the game, and Juliana won.

They hadn't yet been shopping for food so they decided to eat out that night. They decided to walk to a restaurant not the least because they could then drink before they walked slowly back.

Easily, sometimes holding hands and occasionally arm in arm, they strolled towards the centre of the town. They headed towards the Penon, not least because most routes to anywhere in Calpe headed to and from the Penon, but they stopped short and sat down in a fish restaurant, in the open air, drawn to it mainly by the beautiful smell of fish cooking, a strong tangy smell that filled the darkening air as the night came in.

They stayed there for several hours, enjoying the smells of fish mixing with the strong tang of perfumes of the flora around them. As the sun had gone down so the streetlights and myriad of other lights around the town had come on, and in the night, it became a quite different town.

'It feels different,' Mike said.

Juliana nodded. 'It does. Well, it feels completely different but also very reminiscent. Can you remember what it felt like when we were here before?'

'That was forty years ago,' Mike pointed out.

'You're memory's not that bad.'

'But the town isn't the only thing that's different,' Mike suggested. 'I'm different. You're different. We were very young the last time we were here, and now we're ... well, not old ... but certainly older. We've changed. I don't feel the same way about things that are the same. Do you?'

'I suppose not,' Juliana said. 'But in another way, this is taking me straight back to that time. To when we were here. It makes me feel young again.'

Mike agreed with that but, unlike for Juliana, the thought didn't bring him any pleasure.

Calpe 1984

Mike and Maria were spending the day together on the beach, enjoying the sun and the drinks and the laziness. Maria had some stunning outfits and, on another day, Mike would have appreciated the way her swimming costume showed off her curves, but right now he was distracted by last night's revelations.

Juliana was still away. Mike and Maria both knew, had even said to each other, that this was a one-off, or at best a session together of limited time, but Mike had decided to enjoy that time. He had telephoned the villa where she was with her friends and they had had a quick talk.

'I'm mostly with Andrea at the moment,' Juliana said. 'We're just chilling down at the beach and this evening we're going out to a restaurant she says is out of this world. I think we'll be meeting Carrie there too. I'll let you know how it goes.'

'Have a great evening. I'll call you tomorrow and catch up.'

'What have you been up to?'

'I drove down to Moraira. It's quite nearby. Just had a day at the beach and walking around. Had an evening in a bar where I met a couple of guys and we spent time watching the golf on the tv. It was a good evening.'

'Okay. Catch you tomorrow.'

Mike thought back to the end of last night. Maria had said then that she was thinking of leaving Stephen. Mike had thought at that time that she was waxing lyrical about the time they had spent together. He laughed at the time and told her to get a grip. But her reply was a serious one. A serious face and she said it was more than that. But she had said no more. Now, he had asked her what she had meant and her reply had been her comment 'You asked me about the mark on my back.'

'So, what about it?

'I've been going out with Steve for almost two years,' Maria started. 'It was good at first.'

'But not now?'

'I love him.'

'Okay.' Mike could hear that there was conflict in there somewhere. He waited.

'But he's not a very nice guy.'

'Leave him.'

It was a simple suggestion and not a very unique one. But Maria spent a long time, silently, shaking her head. 'I can't,' she eventually said.

She sat forward on her sun-lounger. 'It was really, really wonderful at first. Steve couldn't do too much for me. He always found something special to surprise me with. One time we stayed over in a hotel, just one night, and when I went in the bathroom he had filled it with flowers, petals all over the floor, and floating candles in the bath. When I sat in the bath he turned on the CD player and he'd prepared a whole playlist of music I loved.'

'Sounds special.'

'It was so, so special. Another time we were in bed at his place, and he'd made a whole Picnic-in-Bed meal on trays, with champagne. The best ploughman's. Which he knew I loved.'

Mike stayed quiet, let her go through her memories.

'And he'd organise special cars when we went out. Not taxis, limos. He just made me feel very special.'

'And this all came to an end?' Mike asked.

'No. He still does it.'

Mike shook his head. 'I'm missing something here I think.'

'There's another side.'

'To him?'

She nodded. 'I don't know how to explain it.'

'Start at the beginning and let it flow.'

Maria thought for a bit, and summer up her thoughts. 'It is probably easiest to start when I did the cycling. The ride to Amsterdam.

'You know that I kept back from telling him you were training me. I didn't deny it, I just didn't say much about it. When he asked who helped me I mentioned you but I added a few others. He seemed okay about that. Then when we got close he seemed to be getting uptight about the ride, tried to turn me off going a few times. I stuck to my guns, and we had a few telephone calls where he was … well … checking up on me. And you know I was completely fair; I never wandered.'

Mike thought about commenting on the last days, and decided against it.

'When I got back he laid on me really nice treatment and I enjoyed it. But there was something else inside him, and it started to come out.

'He had done a few changes to my home; nothing I can really point out, but things that were important to me were somehow set aside, and things that were important to him were more forward. I was starting to live in his flat instead of the other way round.' She stopped and pointed a finger at Mike. 'My paperwork,' she said. 'My papers used to end up on the floor and his would be on the little table I sometimes used. It was stuff like that.'

'That doesn't sound so bad,' Mike admitted.

Maria was quietly thinking, and agreeing that it didn't sound that important. 'It developed. Firstly he tried to stop me seeing friends. Sometimes I would see my friends, like Juliana, when he wouldn't know. Then I started to feel afraid. I loved the times we spent together but it could be strained every now and again.

'More recently he has hit me. A few times, he has hit me. And enjoyed it I think.'

'And that is the mark on your back?'

She nodded.

'How did it happen?'

Maria seemed to close in on herself. 'We were having sex. Good sex. Exciting. And suddenly he picked up a hot piece of metal near the bed, and pushed it against me. It hurt one hell of a lot. And it caused that scar. The worst thing about it only occurred to me afterwards. There was no reason for anything like that to be near the bed; he had obviously set it up so that he could do it. He had planned it.'

'You should get away from him,' Mike said, clearly.

'I've left him several times.'

'And he's forced you back? Persuaded you back?'

She was silent again. Eventually she shook her head. 'He doesn't care. He's never asked me back. I don't think he could care less. I always go back to him. If I had to, I'd crawl over broken glass to get back to him. I so wish I didn't. But I can't stop myself. I just can't be without him.'

'If he has proven he can be violent he might not stop, he could kill you,' Mike said plainly.

'I know.'

They sat silently for a while. They ordered more drinks. They left the topic completely and both read sections of the newspaper they had picked up at reception. They even chatted about the news; light political comments, arguments about a women's rights issue that was topical at the time. They ordered more drinks.

Mike didn't know how to raise the subject they had been talking about, or even whether he should or not. It was Maria who raised it. 'I sometimes worry that he will kill me,' she said.

There were a thousand things to add to that, Mike thought, but he couldn't think what to say. Instead, he took the conversation back. 'If he's violent he could kill you. You should get away from him.'

'That's not what I fear,' she replied.

'Well, you should fear it. It's real. If you think even slightly that he could you should get away from him. Everything you've said to me tells me you should run. Run and don't stop. Maybe you should report it to the police, but even if you don't do that you should run.'

'What if I did?'

Mike had no reply to that. He thought it was probably a rhetorical question.

'What if I did?' she said again. 'I'd probably go back to him. I can't keep away from him.'

'He would force you back?'

'I would force me back.'

Calpe 2023

Their first days were refreshingly normal. They spent some time on the beach, had some light meals and coffees and some wonderfully, peaceful walks.

It was on their fourth day that Juliana left Mike on his own. She had already flagged up that she would want to spend some time alone. Mike knew that that could be useful to him, because he had some tasks he wanted to undertake, and undertake alone. But he also didn't want her roaming about on her own because of the things she might discover. Some days he thought that was a pointless fear; that it was forty years ago and there was nothing to find, and some days he remembered that she had started all this and the evidence was, according to that letter he had discovered by her fruit bowl, that she was here because of something inspired by someone else.

The dark side and the light side.

'Don't start all that stuff up again Mike,' was Juliana's hardest comment when he argued with her about her going off alone.

'I wasn't starting anything,' he argued. 'we're only here for a few weeks and I thought you wanted us to spend it together.'

'Why?'

'Because we were here together back then and I thought you wanted to share the memories together.'

'But we weren't together all the time we were here before,' she reminded him. 'We spent quite some time apart if you remember.'

Was there something in her voice that hinted at something? Mike decided not to pursue that too far.

'Okay. Okay. I'm not pushing it.'

'I think it's important that we don't. You remember how things went a while back. What … twenty years ago or around that time?'

'Yes, I do.' She had gone with her friends sailing for the weekend; and came back excited and having had a really enjoyable time. They had had to do all the things that are needed when sailing; climbing the masts to adjust the sails and so on. They had cooked on board and parked the boat next to other boats and learned to get to shore walking across the other boats which was apparently the way it 'worked'. Mike was attracted to her description and they talked, clumsily, about doing it together sometime. Gradually it became a fierce row and Juliana admitted that it was something she enjoyed doing because it was her find, and not his. It was something she had discovered and she didn't want him involved. He understood that, but couldn't feel the way she did. Eventually they put it aside.

'Everybody needs personal space. Everybody needs time of their own, hobbies of their own, space of their own. We nearly came apart back then because, frankly, you didn't get that.'

Later that day he walked down to the beach at Playa del Arenal-Bol and sat there thinking. He couldn't get an angle, but he was thinking back forty years to find one. He looked over to the Penon, and thought about what had happened up there. He looked at it quietly for a while, and then suddenly realised that he was also looking at Vista Maritima, the apartment where they had stayed when they had been here.

'Pardon me,' she said. 'But I'm pretty sure I'm right. Mr Michael Dawkins Isn't it?'

Mike turned towards the woman standing by his table. She wasn't young, but a lot younger than him. Perhaps around 40 or a little under. She was attractive, but he could feel that she was not reacting to him that way. Besides, she seemed familiar but he couldn't place her. He knew very few people out here and she was not one of them.

'Purdey, Mr Dawkins. We work in the same company.'

It clicked. Purdey was the new woman at the office, she had joined just a few months ago, he seemed to remember. 'Well, that's a coincidence,' Mike offered.

'It was almost a shock,' she said, with a smile. 'I hardly know anyone at the office that well and when I saw you just now I was fairly sure I had it wrong.'

'Well, it's good to see you. Are you on holiday here?'

'Yes. I've got a couple of weeks off work. And I know Calpe quite well so I thought I'd take a break here.'

The waiter brought his coffee and laid it on the table.

'Would you like something?' Mike asked.

'That would be lovely,' Purdey replied, and sat down in the chair. The waiter brought more coffee over.

'Are you here with anyone?' Mike asked.

'My husband and our son. But they're away for a couple of days. They travelled up to Valencia yesterday.'

'Do you often take time apart?'

'Not that much. But my husband's mother lives up there and he wanted to take our son up to meet her. They haven't met up for a few years.'

'And you didn't want to go?'

'No.'

Mike felt the lack of a response, and decided not to press it.

'I'm here with my wife,' Mike said. 'Perhaps you'd like to join us for dinner? Or at least a drink?'

'That would be nice. But I have plans for this evening. I met some girls on the plane and we promised each other we would team up and go for drinks. I don't think I can invite you.' She laughed and Mike thought it was either because they were all girls, or they were all a lot younger than him. Or probably both. He bowed, and she laughed.

She finished her coffee and stood up. 'Thank you for the coffee. I hope we'll meet up again sometime. In fact I'm sure we will.' She kissed him lightly on one cheek and walked off.

He watched her go, put down his coffee cup, stood up and slowly walked in the direction of the Penon. He spent a short while thinking about Purdey, and about what a coincidence meeting her had been, but then he diverted over towards Maritima.

Once there he looked around and realised that it was virtually unchanged since he had been there. The pool was different, he thought, but then again, he wasn't sure he remembered it that well. One or two of the apartments in the tall block now had covered balconies that he was sure none of them had back then. But it was so much like it had been when he had been there before it brought back memories that were surprisingly strong. He felt his anxieties rising just standing there.

He walked round to the entrance, which still had no security to speak of, as he remembered from before. He could see that there were security doorbells for each flat, and that there were security gates to the two sides of the block, but the walk through to the swimming pool was as open as ever. He had never seen anybody abuse the pool he had to admit, in fact hardly anybody even from the flats ever swam there or even sunbathed there. He walked through and stood by the pool, looking around.

'disculpe señor, ¿puedo ayudarlo?'

Mike turned to the pool man who was standing beside him, and who had asked the question. He didn't understand and shook his head.

'Senor. Will I help you?' The man said in slightly broken English.

'Not really.' He started to walk away, but turned back. 'Actually, I'm looking for a friend, well … a friend's apartment. She lived here a long time ago and I was trying to catch up with her.'

That was too much for the pool man, but he gestured to ask Mike to stay where he was and walked into the small office nearby. When he came out he was followed by another man, who walked up and shook his hand.

'Good day sir. Mateo said you were looking for someone?'

'Yes. A friend of mine from many years ago. She owned an apartment up there, in fact I stayed in it almost forty years ago, and I was hoping to track her down and see how she was. Since I was here.'

'Well, we have to be confidential about the owners, sir.'

'I understand and I don't want you to break any rules. If there is anything you can offer me, or a direction you can point me, I would just appreciate it.'

The man gestured to him to follow him into the office, saying 'I'll see if there's anything I can do.'

In the office Mike gave him the number of the apartment and he looked up some notes from a file. 'I doubt you'll still have any record that I stayed in there,' Mike offered.

The man laughed slightly, closed the file and gestured for him to follow again. 'I wasn't expecting that. But the people currently staying up there are, I'm sure, also friends of the owner. I can introduce you to them, and perhaps they can tell you who their friend brought it from. But I can't make any promises. If they don't want to talk to you then you must go away and leave them alone.'

'I understand.'

He knocked on the door that Mike remembered from forty years ago, and a young woman came to the door. The official spoke quietly to her while Mike stood back. She pushed back the door to allow entrance, and the official came back to Mike before they went in. 'As I thought, she is happy to speak to you, and they are friends of the owners, but please be brief.'

Mike agreed and they walked in. Mike put his question to her politely but bluntly. 'I stayed here some forty years ago. In this apartment. At that time this block was owned by Maria Kriska, in fact by her boyfriend Stephen I think, and I was hoping to catch up with her. It's been a long time I know, but it would be good to catch up again.'

'It's still owned by Maria. Well, by her family. I think it is now owned by their child. My husband knows more about it, but I'm sure that's right.'

'Do you know if she passed it to him recently?'

'She died I'm pretty sure, I think she left it to him.'

Mike hoped he had managed to hide his feelings; the unexpected news hit him harder than he might have expected. 'Do you know how she died?'

'I think Trevor, my husband, said cancer. But I'm not sure about that. Cancer, I think. My husband's not here at the moment, so I can't help you more, I'm sorry to say.'

Mike left shortly afterwards. He walked back towards the beach and sat down with a coffee. He felt sad that Maria was dead, and he fondly remembered their time together. Some very lovely days and nights.

But it also meant that the other thing he remembered, that he had shared only with her, had also died with her. It was now a secret he alone held. He remembered the old saying that the only successfully kept secret was held between no more than two people, and one of them should be dead.

And he was contented to let it die with her.

Calpe 1984

They had the following day together and put the question of Stephen aside. Mike arrived at her apartment in the late morning. He proudly listed a few things she should bring with her, transferred a couple of rucksacks from his car to hers and together they drove for about an hour, first down the coast and then inland to Guadalest in the mountains. It was only around twenty miles but the road was twisty and turning and full of hairpins.

They didn't drive directly to the village, but turned off into a small unsecured area where a stream was running gently along.

'This is where we stop,' Mike said.

Maria didn't argue or even question. She got out of the car and watched as Mike also got out. 'Am I suitably dressed?' was all she asked.

'No. You'll need your slip-ons. And it's going to be a scorching day so wear an easy top. Something that covers your shoulders and you won't mind getting wet.' Mike himself put his own slip-ons on, his swim shorts and a t-shirt. He packed jumpers and towels for the both of them into a rucksack. 'And pour on the sun cream; it's a hot day and we're going to be out in it most of the time.'

'Can I take anything?'

'Yes, Mike nodded. 'You take this rucksack. It's not heavy.' He handed her the rucksack and she slipped it on her back. Mike took the other, heavier, rucksack and slipped that on his own back.

'Let's go.'

Maria looked around for somewhere to go but had to wait for Mike as it wasn't obvious which direction they would take. Mike stepped down into the stream, held out his hand to steady her as she stepped into the stream, and they walked in the middle of the water, about a foot to two feet deep, against the flow.

It was a beautiful walk. The sun was strong but often hidden by the cliffs either side of them, and they enjoyed the sparkling crepuscular rays twinkling through the overhanging leaves of the trees. The water was warm, and no effort to push through. They passed pine, strong smelling and almost sensual, and mingled with the scents of citrus, olive, carob and almond trees.

After a short, and silent, walk they came to a waterfall in front of them. The waterfall was what was feeding the stream. Mike led them both to one side, and they climbed, without great difficulty, over the rocks under the waterfall. It took around a half an hour, and some parts of the climb were tough but not dangerous, and they emerged at the top of the waterfall where there were a small scattering of people laying in the sun.

'That was really lovely,' was all Maria said. Mike indicated a place where they could sit down, with trees to cover them if they wished, but also plenty of sunlight for sunbathing. Maria stood up and looked across the valley to a lake in the distance.

'The Embassament de Guadalest,' Mike called out to her.

'What's that?'

'That lake you're looking at. It what it's called. It's actually a reservoir but also a lovely beauty spot.'

'I've lived here for years on and off but sometimes you seem to know more about the place than I do.'

'I studied the area a bit last night. I wanted to make today special.'

'You have.'

They sat together and absorbed the atmosphere, and enjoyed not just chatting but hearing the people around them chatting, even though they couldn't hear anything anyone was saying.

'Can we get any food around here?' Maria asked eventually.

'I thought you'd never ask,' joked Mike. He quickly unzipped the rucksack he had been carrying which was set out near them. As it opened Maria could see not only different supplies of food, but also two plates, two plastic but ornate glasses, knives and forks, together with a spread of fruits, cheeses, pate and some chocolate. And a bottle of champagne.

Maria said nothing, but the smile on her face as they quietly ate the lunch together, said everything. They closed on each other and kissed. It felt like something good was developing between them. And silently they both felt the possibility they were getting in deeper than they should, into something they hadn't anticipated.

They shortly afterwards packed up their rucksack, dumped their rubbish in one of the bins laid out nearby, and they walked across the grass, and across the road, and spent a while walking towards a small town ahead of them.

'Guadalest?' asked Maria.

'Yes. It's a bit touristy to be honest, but good to see. I think they say it's the most visited village in the whole of Spain. Do you fancy it?'

She turned to him quite openly, 'I fancy being with you today, wherever you are.'

They stopped just outside the town. There were several donkeys, each with seats covered in comfortable blankets, and they sat on two of them for the short walk into the town.

'It was a tradition in the old days that you could only get to this town by donkey. Nowadays it's just tourism. I suspect they will stop that too soon; I think these donkeys get a bit worn out.'

The town was accessed, as it always had been, through a fifteen-metre-long tunnel called the Portal de San Jose. The Castell was famous for many centuries but came to an end during a huge explosion in 1848. There were still parts of it to walk around. In the town were lovely little shops that Maria and Mike wandered around slowly, enjoying the arts and crafts on display and buying silly little gift items while wondering who they could give them to. They stopped in a café and had cold beers and snacks. Perhaps most memorably they found and examined several strange museums; the salt and pepper pot museum, toy museums and one full of dolls houses, and a cat museum.

They left the village, and walked the miles back to their car, only just beating the sun going down. When they got to the car they threw their backpacks into the back, and flopped, tired, into the car. They kissed, longingly but Mike could feel Maria pulling away. As they drove back before they drove back to Moraira, Mike wondered if Maria was thinking through what had happened. He knew that this might seem like a good point to end the affair if it had to end. Mike felt that it was if they had had a delayed relationship from Amsterdam that might be coming to its natural conclusion.

Even as he absorbed that feeling he knew that there was a conflict in him that he hadn't resolved, His feelings were more alive than he was admitting.

They walked together into the apartment, and at that point all the romantic and ... yes, ecstatic ... thoughts disappeared immediately.

Stephen was standing in the living room.

Mike said nothing at first, but took in the position as he saw it. He immediately felt Stephen's attitude. He could feel that although he had said and done nothing his body was tensing, feeling itself to decide if he could win a fight, and Mike realised he was doing the same thing. Maria looked terrified; as if she knew that Stephen would move to fighting, and that she would be the target.

'What the fuck ...' were Stephen's first words.

Mike was more naturally a peacemaker; he held out his hands to try to cool down the moods. 'Let's take it easy,' he said.

'Steve,' Maria started. 'Just calm down.'

At first Stephen seemed to go along with it. 'Calm down', he said. 'You mean I'm mistaking what's going on here. I'm getting it all wrong.' He smiled, cruelly, and pointed to Mike without actually looking at him. You mean this cunt isn't fucking you? I'm misunderstanding?'

'It's just something that happened. It can stop as easily as it started,' Maria said.

'Not if I have anything to do with it,' Mike said. 'I want to be with Maria. You might as well know that now.' Mike could barely understand the words coming out of his own mouth. So often he remembered that he had no particular position to take, but given an opposition he would suddenly take a view and pursue it strongly. He hoped long ago that he had finished with that nonsense but here he was, doing it again. He had not thought so long-term about Maria; yet here he was pledging his love for her.

Stephen seemed to relax. Mike thought he had gained an element of control; he was quite wrong. Stephen tensed up immediately and moved quickly towards Mike.

'Talking's better than fighting. But I'm here either way.'

'Fine,' said Stephen, and lunged at him.

Maria lost sight of what happened next. Stephen punched and kicked at Mike and Mike first tried to avoid it, but then punched and kicked back with a vengeance. Parts of the room got broken very quickly, and both men were bleeding, if only superficially, from some of the blows. They were clumsy, and they were both trying to be vicious while holding back from too close contact which would make one side's victory all the easier. People rarely fight like they do in the movies; it's generally scrappy and clumsy. And it was this time.

Then, without declaring it, the fighting stopped as quickly as it had started. Both men were apart and breathing heavily. Maria was standing motionless, not wanting to upset whatever testosterone balance had been set up. She was watching both men closely, unsure what would happen next.

'You have to go now,' Maria said to Mike.

'I'm not going anywhere,' he replied. 'Let's have this out right now.'

Stephen seemed ready to pick up the fight again, but it was Maria who stepped between them and held out her hands. 'No,' she said. 'You have to leave now Mike or this will just get worse, and it can only end in the same way.'

'End how?'

'I mean you have to go. You have somewhere to go, and Steve belongs here. It's up to us to sort this out. Me and Steve.'

Mike stopped, and looked into Maria's eyes where he could see her strong determination. He nodded, to her mainly.

He recognised that he was the outsider. But he also felt he couldn't just walk out; the descriptions that Maria had given him earlier made him worry that Stephen would turn violently on Maria if he left and he felt he couldn't move. But eventually he did.

'I'm leaving,' Mike said. 'But I'll be back. I want Maria and you had better get used to that. But you two need to talk.' Stephen said nothing, so Mike turned to Maria. 'You okay?'

She nodded.

'Will you be okay?' Mike stressed again.

She nodded again. Then a very calm voiced Stephen turned directly to Mike. 'I'm not giving up the girl I love,' he said. 'You should go. We have a lot to talk about.'

Mike said nothing, but his hesitation frankly asked the question "Is talk all you will do?" and silently Maria nodded to him again.

Mike was unhappy about the position, but he realised he had reached an impasse where he could do no more at the moment. He walked directly out of the door and outside he listened for sounds in the apartment, but there was silence, and he got into his car and drove off.

That evening he called Juliana but got no answer. 'I went over to Guadalest,' he said to the ansaphone. 'Full of tourists and junk shops so nothing much to tell you. It was a pleasant day, but not memorable.'

Calpe 1984

Mike and Maria kept apart the following day, but neither of them thought much of anyone or anything else but each other. Maria, over that time, concluded that her time with Stephen had to end, and that she wanted to pick up with Mike. Mike was less certain of a long-term commitment, but he did feel that time with Maria was what he wanted for now, and he knew that he wanted to keep her away from Stephen. He also could not dismiss Juliana, he loved her too, and now he was in an awful position of having to choose.

The next day they got together after Maria telephoned him to say that Stephen had returned to London. She wanted to see him. Mike was pleased that Stephen was at least out of the way, and he and Maria could talk the situation through calmly. They had simple hours lolling about by the Mediterranean and enjoying eating, and even more, drinking.

From pretty much anywhere in Calpe the one unmissable site is the Penon de Ifach; the thousand-foot-high rock that is not just the major feature of the town, but a major attraction for the whole area. It juts out into the Mediterranean from the centre, dividing Calpe into a southern section and a northerly section at a ninety-degree angle. Every scene in Calpe is backed by this attraction which has a variety of quite different appearances depending on which view you have. It is a local park and has attractions for all sizes of families. There are walks, climbs would be a better word, in several areas of the rock and some of them are quite hairy.

The first part of the climb, from the base to the artificial cave and tunnel that carries the tourists through to the harder parts of the walks, is so easy a walking area that toddlers accompany their families along there. Such little ones gradually break off as the climb gets tougher and tougher.

Mike plodded back from the ice cream shop with two plastic tubs full of banana-split and handed one of the tubs to Maria. She took it and sat backwards, looking away from the Penon. Mike held a hand up over his eyes to prevent the glare stopping him seeing her.

'Thank you. That is exactly what I needed,' she said.

'Me too.'

Maria skimmed off a chunk of the ice cream and slipped it into her mouth, savouring the cold, sweet flavour slowly as she sucked it down her throat.

'How tricky do you think that is to climb?' Maria asked. Mike looked at where she was looking, but she corrected him, pointing over her own shoulder. 'No. That.'

'The Penon?'

'Yeah.'

'From the look of the families walking up there it must be pretty easy,' he said. 'Look. Look at that little group there; some of those can't be much more than six or eight years old.'

Maria turned around and repositioned her chair so that she could sit back and watch. She agreed about the groups of people they could see.

'Why don't we?'

'Fine. I don't know how long it would take but we've got the rest of the day. Plenty of time I would think.'

They finished their ice creams and strolled along the beach towards the Penon. On the roads they passed shops where they could buy typically tourist things; cheap beach equipment overpriced, bad models of the Penon in all shapes and sizes and, inevitably, more ice creams. After a while they stopped outside a restaurant and sat in the open front and ordered coffee. Quietly they sat and drank them, and ordered two more.

As they walked down the front gradually closing on the Penon they watched the many people, hundreds probably, who were walking up towards it. They started to get the sense that it was something people just had to do when you were in Calpe. As they talked about it, it became something of an adventure. They weren't sure exactly where the climb started, or what the route was, but they had a fairly good idea because from the beach you could see the way everybody walked up. But they could see that beyond the easy stretch was a tunnel a lot of the people walked into, and they had no idea what was on the other side. Was it equally easy? They thought that unlikely. But they could see a lot of elderly, and somewhat infirm people, coming back out of the tunnel so they assumed that whatever was on the other side it wasn't that much of a difficulty. It would be a while before they realised just how wrong they were.

They walked to where it seemed the climb probably started. But no matter how varied they tried, they could find no obvious starting point. They even crossed a difficult stretch of grass and shrub but just found themselves getting nowhere, and they retraced their steps back to where they had started. They were both scratching their heads when a young couple walked past them arm in arm.

'Do you know where you start the climb up that thing?' Maria asked them.

The couple were obviously very familiar with it; they pointed in a completely opposite direction to where Mike and Maria had been walking, telling them to go out of the shrublands they were in and walk round to the left. So, they changed angle and wandered round that way, eventually plodding up the stone walk away from where they had been. Then it became obvious that they were on the approach road.

'Now that we're here,' Mike muttered moodily, 'it's bloody obvious that this is the right route.'

Maria laughed and threw a light stick at Mike, but she added 'I'd have to say a few signposts back there would have been useful.'

They walked together following the obvious route, deciding to keep up with the younger couple they had spoken to before, only to find they were not up to their speed, and they watched them climb out of sight ahead of them.

They walked on up a bit more, slightly more steeply, still left and right around the hairpin bends until they reached the vacant area, already quite high up as they looked back on the town, where the tunnel entrance was. There were no signs, no warnings, or anything and they joined the majority of people as they walked through the tunnel.

The tunnel was incredibly dark, considering it was a bright, sunny day, and at times Mike and Maria felt slightly nervous about tripping or falling over on the uneven ground. There were even times when they literally couldn't see where they were putting their feet, and both decided it must be safe because so many people trod through what was obviously a hand-carved tunnel.

At the end they turned a sharp right where they could see the path leading out ahead of them. It looked no more difficult than the paths they had been on and they strolled, sometimes arm in arm, along the route.

The first climbs were more or less the same as before; perhaps slightly tougher angles, maybe a few times Mike and Maria had to step carefully onto, or even hop over, obstacles. But as they climbed, still following the main group that was ahead of them, the climb took on more problems.

Firstly, the path became a fragmented and narrow place to walk, where it was necessary to lean against the cliff walls to keep balanced. Below them were some long and dangerous looking drops. Finding a route to get from A to B was sometimes a case of having to look carefully up and down the route to find the safest way forward. Then some of the walks were along a path, if it could be called that, where your feet had only two or three inches to scratch along. To make that safer in some of the most serious places, chains had been bolted to the cliff faces, and you edged along barely stepping, and keeping safe only by pulling yourselves along the chains. Probably best not to look down the hundred or two hundred-foot drop below you. They saw a sign in several languages; in English it said, 'The path is very dangerous'.

'Now they tell us,' Mike muttered, and got another small stick thrown at him.

When it flattened off more, and became easier to walk along, they were on the top of the Penon, but the climb up towards the peak was still tough, and now hot.

They persisted, noting that there were a lot of younger, and older, and apparently less fit people strolling along with them without the slightest concern. The very younger people had stopped after the tunnel and turned back, but many of those that had carried on were young and small. Mike still had doubts but it made him feel a bit better.

Eventually they reached the peak. Someone had taken the highest rock and inserted a concrete pillar into it, already old and decaying so that the reinforcing metal supports built into it could be seen. You had to wait your turn to sit on it and maybe have your photo taken, and then give it up for the next person.

After that you could mill around a bit and look down a thousand feet to the town below, and to the ships in the harbour and the tiny skyscrapers.

That was when Mike saw him.

It was just his head at first. He was standing over the other side of the peak from where Mike and Maria were standing. Apparently looking away from them, towards the open sea rather than the harbour which had most people's interest. Mike looked at him hard, unsure it was him. But he became sure it was. Maria was looking back across the

Penon. Mike waited until Maria turned towards him, and when she did Mike flicked his head across to the man. Maria didn't get the gesture. Mike did the same thing more slowly, and she turned to look at the figure.

To her credit Maria got it immediately. She turned back to Mike and slowly, and forcefully, nodded. Obviously, she recognised him too.

Stephen was on the top of the Penon with them.

Mike's plans came apart immediately. He decided to follow him down to the town and then see where he went. Mike realised that he couldn't very well get far from him on the narrow paths they were on. But Maria marched with determination straight over to him and confronted him. 'Why are you following us?' she demanded.

'I'm following you,' Stephen said pointedly to Mike.

'You told me you were in London,' Maria said.

'I lied.'

'Get away Steve. Get away. I need time to be alone, to think about what to do.'

'Alone! You need to be alone? How does that involve him?' Stephen didn't point at Mike, who was watching quietly from a distance higher up, but it was clear who he meant.

'He's just with me. We're just up here together. I get time to think alone. He doesn't crowd me, he lets me think. Look how far away he is; he's not on my back all the time.'

'I've been following you most of the day. You don't seem to have done much thinking alone. You've been up each other's arses all fucking day.'

Mike walked down towards them; he felt he should intervene. He felt he should back Maria up.

'After our meeting, if you want to call it that, I want Maria to know what she wants.' Mike said. 'If she wants you then I'll back off.'

'She wants me so fuck off now.'

Stephen turned towards Mike with clear anger and aggression. He pushed Mike back against the wall and turned to pass him, going back up the path presumably to take an alternative track back downwards. Mike decided to avoid Stephen; this wasn't the place to get into another fight with him. Stephen was further down the route they had climbed up, but there were many routes, and Mike led, and Maria followed, along another route that would divert them across the top of the Penon, to a point further out nearer the sea where they would follow another track.

In a brief period, they could no longer see Stephen, and Mike and Maria stepped down another track albeit no easier. They had several stretches of having to hold onto the metal chains embedded in the rocks, and several times they had to spend a little time working out which of several minor routes to take.

'I'm sorry,' was all Maria said.

'Don't be upset. Did he say if he just changed his mind and didn't go to London?'

'He said he lied. I think he never intended to go to London.'

'So, he intended not just to stay here, but to stay here and chase us around?'

'He didn't say that. He might just have had a bad morning thinking about us. I guess he would.'

'You might be right,' Mike said. 'But I'm sticking to the possibility that he's now here because of us. Watch your back.'

They kept walking, and at one point Maria pointed down the slope where they could clearly see Stephen. He was lower than they were, and further back towards the exit path which would leave to the tunnel. Mike silently pointed along the path they were on. It very quickly turned back upwards, and then went over the other side of the Penon. Probably that would just delay their exit and they would leave after Stephen had climbed down, but it could mean they could find a completely different exit from the Penon which would make the whole 'avoiding Stephen' move easier still.

'It was a clever idea,' Mike said, later.

Maria nodded. They had been walking along the path on the other side of the Penon, chatting as they walked, but gradually coming to the conclusion that there was no other exit; everyone walking on the Penon eventually had to exit through the tunnel. So, although they were now on the far side of the Penon, where virtually no one else was, they still had to walk back round the track to the other side and join the tracks where everyone else was. It was going to make the exit that much longer.

Then they saw Stephen again. This time he was on the path ahead of them, and Mike quickly saw that there was no other path. They would have to pass him. Instinctively, immediately, he thought that Stephen had played them like a harp, and had manoeuvred them to where they were now. Mike became afraid for the first time. Maria's descriptions of him as violent felt much more fearful here in an area with so many perils. He didn't want to share that with Maria; not to share just how frightened he had become.

They walked towards him.

Mike broke the silence first. 'Stephen. You want to argue with us lets go down and get some drinks and talk calmly. Let's be sensible.'

Stephen smiled back, cruelly. 'I don't want to argue with 'us', just you. And I don't need a drink to finish you off.'

Mike and Maria moved slightly closer together and walked side by side towards Stephen. He didn't move at all.

When they got right up to him he still didn't move. Mike saw he was standing at the start of a tight section of track. There was definitely no room for fighting there. Whenever they had encountered anyone else on the walk in a place like that there had been a pleasant and helpful exchange so that everyone helped everyone else to pass safely. That didn't seem likely to happen now. Mike knew that he couldn't pass Stephen without Stephen's help, or at least consideration, and Stephen didn't look as if he was planning anything of the sort.

'Come on Steve, Maria started, 'We need to get down. You first, we'll follow.'

Stephen was still smiling with a seriously sinister look on his face. 'No. You two go first.'

Mike didn't want to call him out, but he was sure that he had bad intentions towards him.

'I want to make sure that Maria is okay,' Mike called out.

'Maria can go down right now,' Stephen said. He stepped slightly aside and held out a hand to beckon Maria forwards. 'But not you.'

'You want to fight up here?' Mike said. 'You know this is dangerous, and now you're being stupid.'

'You could easily have an accident up here,' Stephen said. He looked over the edge of where he was standing. Several hundred feet of nothing was spread out below them. 'Accidents will happen.'

Stephen reached behind himself, clumsily it seemed, but when he brought his hand back to the front it was holding a gun.

'Don't be a dick.' Mike could hear both anger and fear in his own voice. He really had the thought that Stephen was going to find a way to make him fall. Now he knew something worse was underway.

Maria started purposefully towards Stephen. 'You're being stupid Steve. Put the fucking gun away. Use it and you'll have to kill me too, and how do you think you're going to get away with that.' She paused for a moment. 'I'm going to pass by and go down. You want to push me off, do it.'

Mike turned to Maria. 'I don't think you're safe.'

Stephen pushed himself way back to allow Maria to get through. There was an easy route now for Maria to step through, but Stephen was still in a position where after she had passed, he could reposition to block Mike. And Stephen still held the gun in the general direction of Mike.

Maria kept going, and Stephen didn't move. She stepped along the ridge, holding onto the chains, and safely stepped off the other side. Stephen gave a sarcastic little clap, and then moved back into the way to stop Mike getting across.

'You're being silly Steve,' called back Maria. 'This needs to end now. Come through, and then let Mike through. I don't want to have to go all the way down to call the police up here to get us all off. Just pack this in and let us pass.'

Stalemate. The three of them stood in their places and said nothing. Mike was thinking that the longer they delayed the greater the chance that they would be encountered by another person or group and he would be able to get away with them. But on the other hand, he knew they were on an obscure part of the Penon. Stephen seemed determined to try to hold the position, but Mike couldn't work out whether that was to get a better opportunity to harm, or kill, him, or whether it was just that he was enjoying frightening Mike as long as possible. Maria knew that if this mood was going to be broken she would have to do it. But leaving the scene left Mike in danger, but at least she could bring it to an end.

Maria broke the stalemate. 'I've had it with you Steve. I'm going to the police. And if Mike comes to any harm, you'd better enjoy eating paella four times a day because I will make sure you go to prison. I will tell them everything.' She hesitated, trying to catch Mike's eye but he wouldn't take his eyes off Stephen. Finally, she turned and hurried off down the slope, and out of sight.

Stephen seemed to think about it for a while, then nodded, and stepped back aside again to let Mike pass. Mike could see that it would be easiest if Stephen went ahead, but he clearly wanted to force Mike into the vulnerable position. Mike looked around; there was no one else anywhere on their side of the Penon. Out of options and knowing he would have to hold on tight as fuck to the chains, Mike started to move. He was ready to push back if Stephen did attack but he desperately hoped that this was just an over-dramatisation that Stephen was enjoying and that it would soon be over. But he's still got the gun, the thought came unwillingly into his mind, he tried to push it back and focus just on the Penon.

Mike grabbed the first of the chains, holding on with a finger-numbing grip, and edged across.

Stephen moved closer, shaking, and Mike realised his mistake, he couldn't move his hands from the chain, couldn't do anything to stop Stephen if he decided to push him straight off the ledge.

Stephen levelled the gun towards Mike, and still Mike couldn't tell if it was a bluff or if he was willing to follow through.

Maria was walking fast, but as carefully as possible, down the slope, fearing what might be happening above her but out of sight. She walked for about fifteen minutes, looking back to see if either, or both, of them were following but she saw no-one.

Until she did.

She heard what sounded like a shot. She heard a scuffle. And then she saw one of them fall hard down the mountain side, slip twice, almost grab successfully to a chain, but miss and then fall several hundred feet down below her. She heard him hit the side of the cliff, bounce out and hurtle all the way down into the sea below.

It was a weird moment because she couldn't be sure which of the two of them it was. They weren't dressed identically, but she hadn't got a clear view. She thought it was Stephen that must have fallen, but she wasn't sure.

She wasn't sure until Mike stumbled around the corner of the slope above her, and clumsily run towards her, and grab her.

'What the fuck happened?' was all she could say. And Mike just kept shaking his head.

'What happened?' she repeated. She was shaking almost uncontrollably. Mike held her to calm her down, but he realised he was also shaking.

'I think he wanted to kill me. Or maybe just frighten me. But he got it wrong.' Mike was talking fast, but very quietly. 'That was when he made his mistake. Stephen switched the gun from one hand to the other, then turned and pushed me. He pushed me at the moment I was changing my grip and position on the chain. It gave me a movement backwards hard; and Stephen stepped straight into it.' Mike faltered for a moment. 'Even a thousand feet up a rock in Spain, Newton's laws of motion hold true. Stephen lost his balance. He leaned slightly inwards to the wall and grabbed for the chain. But he missed it. He stumbled and started to fall onto his knees. Then he slipped off that part of the track and onto the slightly lower section. I heard a loud bang; I wasn't sure what happened. I could see Stephen slowly falling back.'

Maria interrupted. 'I heard a gunshot. At least I think I heard a gunshot. Did he shoot at you?'

Mike shook his head. 'No, he shot himself. Somehow Stephen had let the gun go off. He shot himself. I don't think he was trying to shoot me, it just happened.' Mike didn't think he would ever get the image out of his mind of the dark blood spreading on Stephen's shirt and the shocked look on his face as he slowly fell down the rocks. 'Then I guess, he lost his footing, slipped out from the wall and fell.'

Maria was open-mouthed with shock. 'How did that happen?'

'I'm guessing he slipped, which must happen here a dozen times a day, but this time, and with his injury, he couldn't recover. I watched as his body crashed down on the edge of the path, knocking him outwards, and sent him over the edge, and down.' Mike paused again, as if to get his breath. He could hear his own voice rising as he spoke, and he recognised he was on the edge of losing control. 'The next time he hit the side of the rock was a hundred feet lower, and the impact pushed him out even further. He fell several hundred feet, hitting the rocks again even harder and then falling all the way into the sea.'

He looked at Maria, who said nothing.

'Even at that point,' Mike went on. 'Probably dead already, he hit the rocks and boulders at the base of the rock. I looked down and saw his body lying there.'

Mike and Maria looked at each other. Mike felt that he wanted to tell Maria that they should lie about this. That they should walk away and pretend they knew nothing about it. No-one was there to see what had happened. People probably fall off the Penon every now and again, Mike told himself. On this side of the Penon there was no-one in the village that would have seen it either. What would happen next is that some ship or someone in the sea would find his body; but they could be well out of the area before that happened.

Unbelievably, up on the Penon above them two other walkers had appeared and were heading in their direction. Mike couldn't tell if they would have seen, or heard, anything or not, but he felt the cold fear of being caught before he had even worked out what he had been caught doing. Mike and Maria walked slowly, and the other two got up to them. Mike waited for them to speak, or to ask questions, but they found a place where they could pass and, with Mike's silent gestures, they passed by with just a smile and went on down ahead of them. Mike and Maria looked at each other, but said nothing.

A few others joined them as they slowly clambered down. There was little talking, and most of the way down the only comments were quiet ones between couples and small groups. Generally, it was a silent descent.

Eventually Mike and Maria got down to the lower slopes just before the tunnel and there they met up with many other individuals coming from several other routes. They all got together and there was a general chatter about the weather and the climb and the views, but nothing sinister. Mike and Maria stayed silent, and they walked back through the tunnel and then slowly as a large disjointed pack down the paved route down to the streets of the village below.

They were walking more calmly now. The shock of what they had both experienced was being brought slightly under control. They just had to keep calm, but Mike wasn't sure if Maria could keep calm. He looked at her, and realised that she was the calmer of the two of them. She had got control of herself better than he had.

Alone, and walking slowly, Mike decided he had to ask Maria what she wanted to do about what had happened. But she just shook her head and said only 'Later.'

Moraira 2023

Mike and Juliana had their own plans and both found it convenient that they both needed separation at around the same time.

Mike left Calpe in the very early morning and drove south to Altea, specifically the Altea Club de Golf. Every now and again his pleasure, for a calm few hours, was to play golf either with friends or alone; he really enjoyed the solitude that gave him.

On this occasion he had received a message to his villa that he was invited to play. He wanted to play but more importantly he wanted to know who had invited him. It was very probably a courtesy afforded him by his normal, UK, golf club but he had to admit that the approach had not been that conventional.

He had been given an early tee time. He drove in, parked, and went to reception to get his card, pay his fees, and collect the hired clubs and the buggy. The course also offered a caddie with all bookings but he had declined that invitation to get that extra time to be alone, and to think. Caddies tend to talk all the time when you're not actually playing and he needed the time to think. Today would be less about improving his game and more about thinking clearly.

'I think we're playing together,' she said. And Mike turned to face Purdey standing slightly behind him.

The manager accepted the position as normal, which it was from his point of view, and led them both to where their buggy was parked, together with two sets of clubs, checked if they needed anything else, and then left them.

Purdey took the driving seat without asking, and drove to the first tee.

'This is never a coincidence,' said Mike. His tone alone told Purdey that not only did he think he had been set up, but that it was not necessarily a good thing.

'I was glad you accepted,' she said. 'I thought you might not have done.'

'Was my accepting a good idea?'

'I know you like golf.'

'How in fact do you even know that?'

'I checked your record at the office.'

'You checked my record at the office,' Mike echoed. 'That tells me a lot. You planned your holiday to meet with me, you set up this game of golf for us, and in fact our meeting on the beach the other day was deliberate, yet you pretended it was not. You're setting me up.'

'You're putting that very aggressively and we are here for a pleasant game.' She smiled. 'Plus I have here something I don't think you'd want your wife to see.'

She got out of the buggy, lined up a shot and hit a successful two hundred and twenty yard drive down the left side of hole one.

Mike watched this, and threatened by what she was saying, felt he had no choice but to play along. For now, at least. He stepped up to the tee but his shot was a disaster. He knew from that, and his trembling feelings, that he was in a sticky corner. Purdey made only a slightly sarcastic comment, and climbed back into the buggy.,

Mike stopped Purdey driving. 'Aggressive is maybe fair. I feel I've been set up and you're not denying it. What I've been thinking these last few minutes is how far back does this go? Did you even get the job so that you could be with me. Just how much are you hunting me down?' She said nothing. 'And you are hunting me down,' he finished.

Purdey didn't answer but drove the buggy to the next tee where they disembarked and walked together back to their golf clubs.

Mike went on. 'And how does all this fit in with the husband and son and the mum-in-law?'

'Not difficult. None of them exist.'

Mike used the moment to think while they set up. It was a short, one hundred and twenty yard Par Three and Mike took a seven iron and missed the green completely, Something he probably had not done for a long time. Purdey lined up her shot, missed the green but only just, she was on the apron to the left. She had missed the protective bunkers he had not even got near. They finished the hole, and drove the buggy to the next tee.

'You are an attractive man, Mike. Why do you think I'm after anything but you?'

'The smart-assed comment about what you could show my wife, for one thing. That was not a chat-up line.'

'It could have been an unusual chat-up line,' Purdey answered, and she leaned towards him and kissed him on the cheek. They got out of the buggy and back to their clubs.

They played several holes together in almost silence. Mike, who could barely stop the shaking in his hands, had never played a worse game. Purdey maintained her unnerving friendliness to Mike, and Mike kept as much distance as possible. There was something too cold and unconnected about her approach to him to suggest he should follow it up. And whatever else she was hinting, she was setting him up with blackmail.

After a few holes Purdey said 'I need to stop I'm afraid. I have another appointment. Would you like to continue without me?'

'No.'

They packed up the buggy and Mike drove them both back across the course and to the clubhouse. They ditched the equipment, changed and met outside.

'You're not telling me what it is you think my wife would not want to see.'

Purdey shook her head.

'And even given that, somehow I suspect you have an unusual motive for this,' Mike said.

He was shocked when she delivered it.

Moraira 2023

Juliana drove out of Calpe towards the north. She took the Avenue Juan Carlos 1 which ran parallel to the sea and gave a wonderful drive between the scented beaches and the less than fragrant salt lake, Les Salines. Eventually the main road becomes a winding road out towards the countryside and eventually she drove into the more northern town of Moraira. She stopped at an isolated, small villa at Platja del Portet. It was a sheltered bay with a smooth, beautiful sandy beach with clear blue waters, being enjoyed by a few more adventurous holidaymakers who could be bothered to drive out of the big towns to find tranquillity.

As Juliana walked along the beach looking at the villas a voice called out to her. 'Juliana.'

Juliana looked around but could only see a woman waving towards her. Juliana looked over her own shoulder in case she was misunderstanding.

The woman waved more vigorously. 'Juliana, over here.' 'It's great to see you at last,' she called.

'Phil?'

They shook hands, and Phil pulled her closer and kissed both of her cheeks. They walked together into the villa. Juliana began to get it, and smiled. 'You're a girl,' she said, unnecessarily.

'I always was.' She laughed. 'I guess that didn't come across to you.'

Juliana shook her head. 'It certainly didn't.' For some time Juliana and Phil had been texting and writing but they had never spoken or met. Juliana had assumed all along that Phil was a guy; it had not occurred to her that she was a 'she'. As she thought about that she realised that it was unlikely that she had missed the clues that must have been there. She said nothing, but she instinctively felt that Phil had deliberately hidden that from her. One more thing to add to the inevitable questions.

Inside, Phil made some tea explaining 'I was told all English people drink tea' which made Juliana laugh, and she drank it gratefully.

Phil sat back and looked more closely at her. 'I have been troubled by this for many years. I had no way to move forward on it. In fact, I almost gave up. No, I did give up. For several years I didn't even think about it. But I suppose it was always in the back of my mind. Then I found the notes I spoke to you about, and they started me thinking again.'

'I understand,' Juliana replied. 'I imagine this has been troubling you for many years. It would me, It would anybody.'

'Did you know your father?' she asked Juliana.

'Yes.' Juliana thought inwardly. 'He only died a few years ago. He was a wonderful father. I think I was very lucky.'

'An achiever?'

'Not particularly. He was a solid man. Provided a good home for Mum and the family. Roof over our heads, food on the table, that sort of thing. Office worker, achieved good promotions and a good retirement. Looked after us.' Juliana smiled as she remembered more about him. 'He always supported me, well, all of us, but I think me especially. He never once asked me what I wanted to do when I grew up, but he would take anything I said and he tried his best to back it. But why do you ask? You don't really know me.'

Phil nodded, her mood quiet. 'I want you to know me. I want you to know why I am who I am. Please go on; tell me more about your father. Please.'

Juliana had questions to ask, but did not feel confident to ask them yet. She went on. 'I remember as a child being really into animals. All animals really, partly because of how lovely and how varied they were, but also because they represented something we could be losing. Even when I was a child, maybe fifty years ago, we were concerned then about the harm we were doing to the planet. Not like we're worried now, but it was still there. I loved reading about the things we could do to protect the planet.'

'And he supported that?'

'Yes, he did. I remember he subscribed to a series of magazines about animals at the time, by two people called Armand and Michaela Denis. I think they were the David Attenborough of the time. They started a magazine called Animals and I think it became the basis of some BBC wildlife projects. I found out much later in life that they cost three shillings each ... shillings were the outdated version of English currency in the 1960s ... which wasn't that dear in those days but at that time Mum couldn't work and Dad only had a basic job and the cost was a thing he had to budget for. But he made sure I got every edition each month, or week maybe, I can't remember. And after you had collected a certain number of the mags you could then buy a sort of lever arch cover to put them in and Dad made sure I had all of those as well. It was never going to be a job for me, or make me any money, or at least Dad couldn't know if it would or not, but he knew I loved them and he encouraged me. I loved him for that.'

'That is a wonderful story.'

'I miss him. I've missed him since he died but thinking of him like this makes me miss him even more.' Juliana was getting really into her memories. 'When I was at school I got very into Geography. And geology and, like all kids, into dinosaurs and stuff, but I somehow got the impression that I needed an atlas so that I could really understand the world as it was.'

'And he bought you one?'

'He bought me the biggest and most detailed atlas I have ever seen. I still have it today at home. The countries are very out of date now, particularly Africa, but the physical aspects are still valid for the most part. I still use it now and again. But that wasn't the special part; what was special was that I found out, after he had died, that it was so expensive that he had had to buy it on H P. That's hire purchase, where you pay for it each week a little bit at a time, because he couldn't afford it all on his wages of the time. But rather than let me down, as I suppose he saw it, he made sure that I could get it even if it cost him.'

'He sounds wonderful. Was your Mama also that supportive?'

'Oh yes. She always made it a rule that he had to do the official stuff, he had to sign the cheques and make the big decisions, but I know now that behind him she was fully backing him. I had the two most wonderful parents I could have ever wanted. But I have to ask again; what is it about me that you want to know?'

'No, I want you to know about me. I envy you.'

Juliana came back to the present, put her head down and said just 'Why?'

'I never knew my father.'

'No. You told me.'

'Imagine what that means. Imagine if you had never known your father. I don't mean the things he bought you. Not the atlas, or the animal magazines. But if you had no memory of that wonderful upbringing you had. How much more empty would you feel?'

'I'm beginning to see your point.'

Phil went on. 'He died before we were born. And I would have loved to know him, and to know what he could have been to us. But I never did. I never knew him. But you did. You can perhaps give me a tiny bit of that missing time.'

'I didn't know him well, but I knew him.'

'What can you tell me about him?'

'Can I ask? You said 'we' a couple of times back there. Do you have a brother or sister? That was something I didn't know. Sorry to be nosey.'

'Not really. There was also Charlie. We were twins, but Charlie died at a very young age. There is only me. Sorry to have confused you.'

Juliana shook her head. 'None of my business really, but finding out Maria had a daughter was something of a shock, finding out there were twins is even more of a surprise.'

Phil shrugged, and smiled.

Juliana thought back to where this had started. Decades after her visit to Calpe with Mike and only a year or so ago, she had received a letter from Phil asking if she was the person who used to work with Maria at Styl in London. She had no idea who he was … up to now she always thought of him as a 'he' … but she was keen to catch up again with Maria who she hadn't seen for many years. That turned out to be an unlucky thought; Phil told her that she had died some years before.

Nonetheless Juliana was happy to help out her 'son' if she could and they had corresponded since. A few letters, every now and again, between themselves. Nowhere in that correspondence did Phil even suggest she should keep their letters secret, but Juliana never mentioned it to Mike. It wasn't a secret, it didn't seem something to be secretive about, but it felt right for Juliana to have something to herself and not be shared. She and Maria had worked at Styl, not Mike, and it felt good to keep that, not secret, but to herself.

'Very little to be honest Phil. I worked with your mother. I didn't, to be very honest, know her that well either. We worked together for a few years in a fashion shop in London. In fact, I knew her better in the years before that when we were a couple of girls growing up. But time passes, and we grew up, became a bit more distant.'

Phil nodded silently.

'She told me about her boyfriend and I met him briefly a few times but never really to know him. I'm sorry if that's a disappointment.'

'But you met him?'

'He popped into the shop a few times but we hardly spoke.'

'Mama rented out the apartment to you didn't she. She and Dada. Years ago.'

'Almost forty years ago. Yes. It was one of my first real foreign holidays. We came out here, me and Mike, my husband, before we were married then.'

'Dad was here also.'

'So I understand. But we never saw him. He didn't visit us, and in fact during that time I hardly even saw your mother who was staying somewhere else. But of course, we spoke to her after … it happened.'

'After he died?'

'Yes. Your mother was understandably shocked. She visited us a few days after it happened and told us. It was tragic.'

'Do you know if he fell off that mountain down there?'

'The Penon de Ifach. Yes. I understand that he was climbing around on it, I don't know if he had friends with him or not. But he fell, and he died. I gather they have similar accidents every now and again up there. I've never climbed it, but I've heard that it is hard and dangerous. He was unlucky.'

'He was perhaps more than unlucky?'

'In what way?'

'When he died they found he had been shot. He might have died before he fell, the shot might have killed him. In fact, he might not have fallen at all, he might just have fallen back when he was killed.'

'I did hear about that. But if I remember, the police were sure back then that he had shot himself. He had a gun with him. And they seemed sure that he had shot himself accidentally.'

'So they say.' Phil sat back quietly for a time, and Juliana didn't want to interrupt her.

She seemed to distract herself for a while, asked if Juliana would like something to eat and they agreed on some sandwiches which Phil prepared for them. She made some more tea, but poured herself a glass of wine. As they ate their sandwiches, Juliana also asked for wine.

Phil put down her sandwich. 'My mama told me that he had a bit of temper. More than that; she said he had a very bad temper.'

'I don't know about that. For that you would have to depend on what she said. But don't over-judge him; she knew him day in and day out and she might have had a view of him that you wouldn't have had.'

'I'm not trying to protect him or his reputation. I just want to know. But I keep asking myself why he had a gun with him at all.'

'I don't think that was because of his temper. Don't think that.'

'Do you know why he had a gun?'

'No. I think your mum said at the time that he was probably up there shooting birds or something, He might just have been showing off; young men in particular used to do that I'm sure you know. I'm sure they still do.'

'Yes. Mama told me that too. And that could be right.'

'But?'

'I've always wondered if there was more to it than that. If he got shot by someone else. Killed by someone.'

Juliana held her hands out, shocked. 'Oh God, I didn't know you were thinking that. That's not what we thought at the time. Your mum never suggested even once that she thought that was the case. And the police seemed sure that the gun was his own. You should accept that.' Juliana caught herself as she saw the hurt look on Phil's face. 'I just mean you might sleep easier if you accept that rather than look for bogeymen in the dark.'

That took some explaining and Phil lightened up for a while as she got the explanation. 'I think I do accept it. But he was my dad. I want to be sure. How do I get to be sure?'

'It was forty years ago. What happened, happened.'

'If dad was here when you were here, he might have seen one or both of you. Perhaps not you, but maybe your husband?'

'I'm pretty sure not.'

Phil was still looking down at the ground when she muttered. 'I don't think that's right.'

Moraira 2023

Purdey took her purse from the golf buggy seat and extracted a polaroid photograph.

He took the photo out of her hand and felt his whole body go cold.

Purdey nodded and straightened her shoulders. 'Something I found a while ago. I know about your … relationship … is that what you'd call it? And your wife doesn't know.'

Mike was shocked. 'This is blackmail,' he said. He had not expected to ever see that photo again. Having his secret revealed was one thing, but having it revealed in so sordid a way was a shock.

'I don't know why it was kept. I imagine Stephen's girl, Maria, found it amusing. She probably shouldn't have kept it, but she did for some reason. She used it as a bookmark, I think. I assume because it was humorous. Or romantic. Probably meant to get rid of it, but forgot, or planned to do it later, or whatever.'

Mike looked again at the photo of himself apparently wearing wings that were those of an angel statue behind him, stark naked, and with his cock pointing at the photographer.

Whoever Purdey was, it was clear she really did have the information for her blackmail.

Mike stalled, still reeling from the shock of seeing that photo again 40 years later. 'What are you hoping to gain from this?'

'Money,' she replied simply. 'I have information and I need money. No, to be fair, I don't need the money. I can get the money and I want it.'

'What the hell do you know? I'm not sure of your age but you can hardly have been born when it happened.'

'Let's just say that Stephen's family are looking into this, and I got it by accident. That's all you need to know.'

Mike decided to take time to think this through. He told Purdey that and left with no protest from Purdey. She clearly knew the strength of her position.

Calpe 1984

Still shaking from their experience on the Penon, Maria and Mike got home and both thought they should talk about what had happened but neither of them did. They both knew that there was a possibility they would be at odds with each other. Mike was sure that Maria would want to open up and confess all. And after all no-one had killed Stephen; he had fallen. But Mike wasn't sure that he could trust the Spanish government to treat him fairly. He could easily be blamed for what had happened.

The gun was the problem. How could Mike be sure that the police would accept that it was an accident? Stephen had taken a gun with him to threaten Mike and Maria at the very least, and possibly to kill Mike. Would the police accept the story that Stephen brought the gun? Why not Mike? Could it not look like Mike brought the gun and shot Stephen; in fact, would that not look more likely?

Where was the gun, was one crucial question? If it was still in Stephen's hands when they found the body that would help, but the chance of that was miniscule. Almost certainly it had fallen separately. And it could well be found. And it would probably look as if Mike had thrown the gun away after shooting Stephen to avoid it being seen by others on the Penon.

They spent a while together, and Mike waited for Maria to speak first. He had to know what she was thinking. If she went to the police to confess all at least he would have a witness to his story.

But what if that wasn't the case? He also feared that Maria could still turn to Stephen's side. She wouldn't lie, or blame Mike, he was sure of that. But she could make the conflict between them too even-handed and the police could well take a view that he was at least partly responsible.

And Mike knew that Maria would be suffering the loss of a man she loved. Heaven only could tell why she loved him, but Mike knew she did. Now she was having to side with, at best, a new love while mourning an older one.

In the end Mike decided to wait and see what happened next. But nothing did happen, and the afternoon passed by uneventfully.

They put on the news but nothing was said, even on the local stations. They didn't exactly go to bed so much as fall asleep watching the tv. In the morning they woke up with the news still on and nothing came up then either.

Nothing was covered on the news and Mike started to think that perhaps his body had been washed out to sea and lost. That could solve a lot of problems, but how would Maria deal with that? Mike didn't feel that she would just leave it at that.

They walked together along the front, back towards the Penon, and stopped for a coffee along the way. Still neither of them had said a word to each other about what had happened. They had hardly spoken at all, just irrelevancies about breakfast, the coffee, and a mention of the weather which had, in fact, not changed even slightly since the day before. Once or twice one of them had looked away from the Penon to the other, inviting a comment, but neither said a word.

On the front, nearest the entrance to the walk up the Penon, there were a few members of the Guardia Civil; the national police force. Mike did not know the divisions of the Spanish police but he felt sure that if there was a crime suspected these were the officials who would consider it. They were addressing different members of the public, and Mike assumed that Stephen might be the point of it; as they had seen no Guardia Civil anywhere before. It was too much of a coincidence.

And so it was.

Maria and Mike hovered around the edge of the groups of people and picked up that there was an investigation into a body found at the base of the Penon earlier that morning. People were basically being asked if they had seen anything, if they had been up on the Penon the day before, or if they knew anybody that had been.

Mike looked around as carefully as he could to see if there were any cameras that could have viewed them climbing the day before. He couldn't see any, but it was a tourist area and many tourists would be photographing the Penon.

He thought it would be worth denying having been up there. But he heard one of a group saying that they had been asked if they had any private footage that would be given to the police. And it occurred to him that if they could collect enough footage they would probably be able to monitor the many people who had been up there.

Mike was trying to edge them away from the Guardia when one of them walked directly to them and blocked their walk.

He spoke in Spanish and when Mike indicated that he knew no Spanish he changed to English, though broken. He gestured towards the Penon. 'We are wanting to find out if you were up there the day before,' he said.

Mike was struggling to quickly come to the best position. Admit he was up there or not? He didn't get a chance to answer. Maria spoke fluent Spanish and engaged in conversation with the Guardia officer, who was clearly happy to speak to someone in his own language. For Mike, the problem was he didn't know what Maria was saying and if later asked to agree or confirm anything, he had no idea what he should, or shouldn't, agree to.

Once or twice either Maria, or the officer, directly gestured towards him, but it seemed they were referring to him rather than including him, and he was not asked to contribute.

The talk seemed to go on longer than he had expected, and certainly hoped. He wanted to have an input into what Maria was admitting to, or denying, but he knew that already that had gone too far, and he had now to follow whatever she had decided on.

The talk came to an end. The Guardia officer was polite and wished Maria goodbye. He acknowledged Mike, saying in English, 'My good thoughts to you too.' Then he walked towards other people, and Maria took Mike's arm and gently walked him away.

'I have to ask …' Mike said.

'What we said?'

'Obviously. What did he want to know?'

'If we had been up on the Penon yesterday. If we saw a man he described to me, obviously Stephen. If we saw anyone with him.'

'What did you say?'

'I told him we were up on the Penon yesterday. Loads of people are up there every day. Being there is not the end of the world.'

'What about Stephen?' It was time to get up with Maria.

'I told him he was trailing us, that he attacked us but that you had the last laugh. You pulled out a gun and shot him, and then pushed him off the Rock.'

Mike looked at her with no thought at all in his mind. A compete blank.

She laughed. 'Of course I didn't, you idiot. I told him we hadn't seen anybody like that. I played dumb.' Maria visibly calmed down and

Mike saw that her humour was a way of getting passed what must have been a tense time.

Mike just nodded. He threw out a wan smile and got much the same back. He breathed again. He couldn't bring himself to laugh though. 'And that's it?'

'That's far from it I would think. Eventually they will produce photos of him, and then I will have to recognise him as my friend. There will be too many camera shots of us together. I will have to be shocked and horrified at what has happened to him.'

'Can you do that?'

'I'll have to.'

'We're in this together.'

'No, we're not.' She turned to face him directly. 'You're not in this at all. Stephen must have encountered some thug, given his nature that wouldn't be difficult to believe. And Stephen must have pulled a gun on him, and shot himself by accident.'

'They'll never believe that. I guess the gun wasn't in his hand when they found him?'

'No, it wasn't. But several rounds of bullets were in his pocket. They know it was his gun. They're working on the assumption he shot himself rather than he was shot. They're unsure if he committed suicide, which they doubt, but they think he picked a fight and lost out. Not too far off, in fact.'

'Do they know I was up there too?'

'They don't know. I told them we knew each other a little; that I had rented out an apartment to you and that we occasionally saw each other in town, but that we didn't know each other that well. He seemed uninterested in you. I left it just like that.'

'That's true too. It's a little weird how this is working out.'

'The truth actually working, you mean? Yes, weird indeed.'

'Can you pull this off?'

'I think so. The important thing is the bullets in his pocket; that has taken a lot of the pressure away. If Columbo, or Sherlock Holmes, turn up I'm sure they'll spot the errors and pin us down. But life isn't like that. Sherlock Holmes won't turn up. This could pass by.'

They walked silently together, both thinking about the implications of what was happening.

'What happens when they bring you his photo? How are you going to play that?'

'I think I will be shocked, and I will say that I hadn't realised it was him when I was first asked because I was sure he was away from here. He had told me he was returning to London after all. I haven't yet worked out if I should say he was violent, and that he beat me, but in the end I think they might conclude it was all his fault and his own accident. I hope.'

'Then we are in this together. That works for us both. If it works its perfect.'

Maria stopped and squarely faced Mike again. 'No, we can't be. If it doesn't work one or both of us could end up in prison. But if it works it passes by calmly. And we get on with our lives.'

'Exactly.'

'Separately. We get on with our lives separately.'

'Why?'

'If they work out that we were together, and up there together, then it changes their whole thinking. And I've lied already. The lie should work. But if it doesn't and they can backtrack then we're both in the shit.'

'So …?'

'We both know what happened between us. I know that we had the affair that we might have had in Amsterdam. I wanted it. I think you wanted it back then. Now we've had it. But this is where we should accept that and I must go on alone, and you must go back to your wife.'

Mike knew she was speaking very sensibly, but he wasn't the sort of man who could make broad decisions easily. 'I don't know how…..'

'We walk away from each other from here and we stay apart. You don't tell your friends about seeing me. I guess you weren't going to anyway. And I didn't spend any time with you, apart from maybe a casual drink. And that's it.'

Calpe 2023

Mike stayed slightly behind Juliana as they walked into town, heading for a meal and some wine. They had had a good day, but were hardly talking much. Just both doing some reading, and tidying up the villa.

They stopped at a restaurant they both knew, where good plates of both meat and fish could be had. Juliana fancied fish as often she did, but Mike had said he wanted a good steak. They started with wine, both drinking red despite the fish, and they were through half a bottle before they even ordered the food.

'I was in Moraira,' Juliana offered. Mike had asked a couple of times where she had been, but she had ignored the question. It was time to give some answers.

'What was there?'

'Someone I wanted to meet.'

Mike guessed immediately that it was the man who had sent her the letter he had read by her fruit bowl back in England. He said nothing.

'Her name is Phil,' she added.

'Her?'

'Yes. I had thought he was a man but apparently not. She's a woman.'

'Do I know her?'

'No. She's been writing to me, and we have had a couple of texts. I met her in Moraira for the first time.'

Mike felt comforted by that; it seemed she was openly filling in the gaps, 'Who is she?'

'Maria's daughter.'

'Maria?'

'Maria who rented us the apartment back in the 1980s. My old friend who you cycled to Amsterdam with.'

'I didn't know she had a daughter. Was she there too?'

'She died a while back.'

'What did her daughter want?'

'She wants to know about her father. She never met him, and she hoped we could tell her things she wanted to know.'

'Why would we know her father?'

'Her father was Stephen. Maria's partner when we were here back then. She was apparently pregnant when she was here, though I didn't know it at the time, and Stephen was the father, though he died before his daughter was born.'

'I didn't know she was pregnant.'

'At the time I don't think she did either. The girl was born after she returned home, I think. I didn't remember her and maybe I never knew about her. She left Styl shortly after we got back, and I left not long after too.'

'Styl?'

'The shop I used to work in down in Chelsea. She left pretty soon after we got back. I think I felt she might have left because of what had happened to Stephen. Losing him like that must have been a pretty awful shock.'

'I suppose so.' He paused for a bit. 'Were you able to help her?'

'I don't think so. I hardly knew him, but she knew that. But she wanted to know if anyone else knew him.'

'Anyone else?'

'You, I guess.'

'Me?'

'Yes.'

'Why? It's possible that you would know him, but less likely I would.' Mike thought about it, feverishly trying to catch up with where Juliana was taking him. 'No. I can't recall ever meeting him either. I suppose I might have done if he was at the shop with you and I was there. But it doesn't ring a bell.'

Juliana said nothing, just waited for Mike to speak more.

'It doesn't leave her with much to hope for,' was Mike's only offering.

'When I was with her, Phil showed me some papers. They had been worrying her ever since she found them, and it was only recently that she found out more about them.'

'What papers?'

'Maria had written some … well, let's call them notes … and Phil found them. She read them but she didn't discuss them with her mother until much later. I suspect that she talked to her about them when she found out that she was dying. She would have realised it was her last chance.'

'What …. notes?'

'Diary entries. Diary entries about a lover that she had taken. Notes to herself I suppose. It would seem to have been a short affair she had. She wasn't married, and she had had a few lovers. Everyone does. We were all young; it was hardly anything that extraordinary.'

'Yes?'

'But it seems she had the lover here in Calpe. For maybe only a few days or a week or so. I don't know the details of what Phil found in the letters, but that is what she wants to know more about.'

'Why would we know about him? You might I suppose, having worked with her, but did you?'

'The lover she had was here. In Calpe. And at the time that we were here in the apartment. For some reason Phil thinks we might know more about him, and that's what she wants to know. If we can fill in some information for her she feels it will help her … Well, help her to understand her father.'

'Is that all?'

'All? That's an important thing. She never knew her father and as she gets older she wants to know. Her father. Her roots. Her background.'

Mike said nothing else, neither did Juliana. But Mike could feel, strongly, that she was holding something back.

Calpe 2023

Mike kicked a small clump of sand away from his foot and then buried his toes into the sand near his lounger. He picked up his book again, for the umpteenth time, and sat back. He took a moment to check that Juliana was still reading her book; it would give him time to think.

He had been listening to her concerns for Phil and sympathising openly, but seething internally. He wished she could just drop the bloody thing and they could get on with their lives. It was over forty years ago, for heaven's sake. Her father had been dead forty years, and her mother was now dead. Phil had never known her father; this was a poor time to start worrying about it, he thought.

But he heard what Juliana had said; that she wanted to know her own roots, her own background. And he understood that. He agreed with it, or he would have done, if he hadn't also known that he had a lot to lose.

'You knew your father, your parents,' Juliana said, putting her book aside. 'Imagine if you didn't. Imagine if you couldn't feel your own past. You did something, or felt something, or believed something and you couldn't realise why. That you knew it came from your own background, but you couldn't feel where, or why....'

'I would just put it aside. There are things you just can't get back to.'

'You wouldn't do it that easily. You'd try.'

'Plenty of people are in no better position. Their fathers and mothers, maybe both of them, die when they're young. There must be many who never knew either of their parents. They get by in life.'

'But they know where they come from. They know who their parents were. They can ask other relatives. About their own younger life. And about their parents. And more.'

'But they don't get an accurate picture. They just get someone else's ideas of what they were, or how they lived ... '

'No one has an accurate picture. You don't even have an accurate picture of your own life. Neither do I. Neither does anyone.

You remember your own life as you want to, or maybe bits of it even as you didn't want to ….'

'That's what I mean. So, what's the point?'

'The point is that you still have a picture. It may be inaccurate, but you have a picture you can live with, or challenge, or argue against. But she doesn't. Her mother kept a lot from her. She doesn't know what her father was like. And with her mother dead she has few channels. But she's trying. A lot of what we think are our memories are actually from photos. Your mum or dad keep photos and you look through them and ask and then that becomes a memory. Things not photographed fall into nothing. We don't know how much we don't know. But Phil does know. She knows nothing and she knows that. She hasn't got any photographs of herself with her father because there aren't any. She's desperate to put something together.'

'Probably she doesn't even know if this lover of her mother's, assuming she even had one, is her father. She doesn't even know that.'

'Don't shout.' Juliana held her hands out passively. 'You're getting the whole beach agitated. Cool it down.'

Mike sat back, realising he had been getting more and more agitated. He picked up his book and looked at it for a while before realising he hadn't remembered a word of what he had read. Then he threw it down and looked around for something else to do, rather than go on with this.

'If we can help her, we should,' Juliana said gently.

Mike was having some trouble concentrating on Phil. Juliana did not know the struggle he was dealing with about Purdey, and that was something he was not going to share with her. But frankly it was more prominent in his mind than Phil.

'Why. She's nothing to do with us,' was the best he could offer. To try to get rid of this nonsense.

'I knew her mother. I worked with her and we came here because of her. And anyway, I don't need a reason. If I can help her why wouldn't I? It doesn't cost me.'

'Maybe it does cost us. We're getting involved in someone else's problem.'

'Then back away and do nothing, But I'm not going to. Understand? Get that? I'm not going to.'

'Okay, okay, if you insist then let's at least do it together.' Mike saw that if she was going to go burrowing into the past he should be

125

there to burrow with her. At least he would know if she found anything. 'But do we know anything anyway?'

'We know she had a lover. Here. In Calpe. Her own notes make that clear.'

'Was she a faithful person?'

'What do you mean?'

'Did she have a lot of lovers? We were all very young in those days. And it was just after the new freedoms of the pill, and youth coming out, and women's lib and all that. What was she like back then?'

'She could well have had other lovers. But I doubt she had any others out here.'

'Well, she had one. She was with Stephen you say she talked about another one. That sounds fairly promiscuous.'

Juliana said nothing.

'She had such a lover here, not Stephen, and it was passionate enough to make her record some personal diary notes. That says something.'

'Not necessarily. I think the way Phil described them they were notes written by her mother, by Maria, to her lover but never given to him. She described them more as diary notes. She was describing her feelings to him. But she may never have given any to him.'

Mike absorbed that quietly.

'Can we see the letters? It might give us some idea about the type of man she was seeing. I guess he must have been a local. She came out here often I seem to recall. She probably met up with someone and saw him now and again when she stayed out here.'

'Maybe.'

Mike waited for her further agreement, but he didn't get it.

'No. This seems to have been a sudden one-off guy. Someone that she came across at the time. It maybe only lasted a couple of weeks or so. That's what Phil felt when she read them.'

'Didn't they even give a name? If she was writing a personal diary of sorts why didn't she name him?' Mike was testing, and he knew it. He hoped she didn't.

Juliana shook her head. 'Apparently not. Phil thinks maybe she had good reason not to mention him.'

'What reason?'

Juliana skipped past that one.

'Phil said some of her memories, in her letters, were very vivid.'

Vivid?'

'Sexually. Almost pornographic. From what she described they weren't the memories of a couple who had spent a long time together. Who had got to know each other over time. She said they were the memories of the short term. I don't think she described it very well, but I got the feeling she meant that she was describing lust rather than love.'

'Well good for her,' Mike said off-handedly.

That triggered something in Juliana who turned squarely to face him. 'It's not a matter of something funny.'

'I didn't mean that,' Mike said, drawing back. 'But if she chose to have an affair I'm glad it was good for her, even if it meant her relationship with Stephen wasn't so good. But I can see how that might upset Phil.'

'It was a long time ago,' Juliana agreed. 'I don't think that is troubling her now.'

'Something else?'

'I don't know the details of what Phil is reading. But part of it concerns how her father died.'

'In what sense?'

'Phil wants to know if it's possible that her father was killed by someone.'

Calpe 2023

It was a couple of days later that Juliana went over to Moraira and met with Phil again.

Phil pushed the piece of paper across the table, and Juliana picked it up.

'How much of this is there?' she asked.

'Not that much I suppose,' she replied. 'Given that it is all I really have of my parents you could take the view that it is very little, or an entire world. I don't think she was with this guy for very long.'

'Do you resent your mother being with him?'

The directness of the question took Phil by surprise. She started to reply several times, but each time faltered and thought more. 'No,' she eventually admitted. 'I think I have done ever since I first read these papers. But not anymore.'

Juliana waited. There was clearly more to come; she could see in her eyes.

'She was my mother, and Steve was my father. Even though I never knew him I have grown up respecting him. When I was young, younger, he was my hero. No more, I suppose, than any other child thinking of her father. I just grew up that way, and when I discovered that my mother had had an affair I was bitter. Angry. And hurt. But it's more complicated than that isn't it? She is still my mother, and she must have had needs and desires. When I thought about it I realised I had looked at it with child-like eyes, but I have also grown up. I've had several relationships and they overlap, and they all mean something different. I saw it through my mother's eyes as an adult. I had to accept what happened.'

Juliana still said nothing.

'I don't know about my father. I think there were suggestions that he might have been a bit of tough guy. It was easy to think of him that way very positively, but again grown up eyes see the complexity more. He could have been difficult to be with. In any case it could have just been a fling that ended at an inconvenient time. It's a long time ago. And also, well, maybe I've got older and more tolerant… Less angry. I look at what my mother did with more of a smile, knowing I've done the same and virtually everyone I know has too.

'So, I don't think I resent the fact that my mother had an affair even though I'm sure it upset my father. I think they would have kissed and made up and put it behind them. Had he lived. But that was the thing that changed it all; they never got the chance to put it behind them.'

'I think that is very wise,' Juliana said. 'Wiser than a lot of people would be who are older than you.'

'But I would still like to know who the other man was,' she said, with a slight edge of hardness.

'Does it matter?'

'It could. Bear in mind that my father died not from falling off that cliff, or not only that anyway. He was also shot. I want to know that he wasn't shot by anyone else. I want to know he wasn't shot by her lover.'

'The police didn't think so.'

'They dismissed it as unlikely. But they were also closing a case and the world is full of policemen who are a bit quick to do that. It could have just been they thought it was the simplest way. Even if they were doing their best, it doesn't mean they were right. Could a clever killer have outwitted them?'

'I know you have to know the truth. But I really think it was some sort of accident. The police were very impressed by the fact that he was shot by his own gun which he was holding when he fell. He had bullets in his pocket that were his. Maria thought he might have the gun for sport, shooting birds or something.'

'Suppose the killer got to his body and planted the bullets, and even the gun?'

'Maria told me she thought he had a gun. She told me just a few days after he died. She visited us not long afterwards. And I also heard that the body was found quite quickly; If the killer, as you put it, was up on the cliff I don't think anyone had a chance to get down quick enough to reach him.'

Phil nodded. 'I thought for a while that any killer could have had an accomplice waiting down the bottom.' She smiled. 'But I got over that a while ago. I'm not a conspiracy theorist. I could be the only person in the world who thinks J F K actually was shot by Lee Harvey Oswald.' She smiled. 'No. I don't think anyone else was involved. But you have to think that my father was here, her lover was here, and my father died. Even if it was not murder, there could easily be a connection.'

'I understand that.'

There was a silence during which time Juliana read the paper she had been passed. It was a succinct note, a couple of hundred words at the most, and just describing a time when Maria and her lover had been at home together one evening. It described the cooking, the wine they drank, and the sex they had had. It was short, but blunt and graphic. Juliana looked at Phil to see if she had a reaction, but she was smiling.

'I know, I know,' she said. 'I am glad she had a fun sex life. I've grown up enough to see past her being my mother sometimes.'

Juliana and Phil shared some wine, and snacks that she had laid out. They sat outside in the evening sundown, chatting easily. She passed her other notes, some shorter and some much longer, and she read through them as they talked. Sometimes she would pick up on something and ask her about it. Often, she could amplify a point from discussions she had had with her mother, sometimes she had to admit she didn't know the answer.

They read through and chatted about the trip they had taken to Guadalest.

'That troubled me more,' Phil admitted.

'Why? It seems they had a very good day.'

'I agree. But that day has troubled me. I said I didn't have a problem about my mother having an affair with this guy. But I think that day may be the day they fell in love. I am sure the way she wrote about it is more than friendship, or lust. I think perhaps she fell in love with him that day, and perhaps he did also.'

'That troubles you?'

'Yes. Not because of his death or anything. Just … I suppose … just because I still want to know my mother and my father were in love all their time together even if she was being naughty. And that tells me maybe … well … maybe if he hadn't died shortly afterwards they might have split up.'

'I see that,' Juliana agreed.

'If that was true I suppose I could accept it. Life moves on as we've said a few times. But that spoils one of my fantasies.' She smiled, but coldly.

They read other notes written by Maria. Maria and her lover hadn't been together that long, but she seemed to have jotted down almost everything they had done in that short time. Days like Guadalest were obviously meaningful, and a dinner one night. She had recorded just sitting having coffee and listening to music, and described the music in detail, and what it had meant to her.

They had even played some table tennis, and she had recorded, somewhat clumsily, the scores. Juliana was amused that there was a broad note at the bottom 'I won!!' with a smiley face drawn after it.

Calpe 1984

Mike was sitting on the balcony, sipping a glass of wine, when Juliana arrived. She looked tired, but happy to be back and, even more than that, happy to have the rest of the holiday ahead.

'How was it?' Mike stood up and helped her put her bags down. He poured her a glass of wine.

'Good,' Juliana said as she sat down next to him. 'It was good to see them, but I'm glad I'm back.'

'Tell me about it.'

'It was just the usual. Carrie drunk a lot and Andrea apologising for her.' She laughed. 'You don't want to hear about it. What about you? Did you find things to do while I was gone?'

Mike muttered some pointless things about walking on the beach and so on, but quickly got Juliana next to him at the table, a couple of bottles of wine in full flow, and the chatting random and excited.

'Come on, give me more details,' Juliana said.

Mike stretched back into the things he had rehearsed. 'The last day was the most interesting. Before that I visited Moraira and Guadalest, which is the most visited town in Spain I heard and I can believe it. But yesterday I drove down south and visited the Punic Rampart which is about two thousand years old. Looked at a few Roman ruins. There was theatre and a museum which I can't remember the name of, and the Roman Colonnade, the House of Fortune, and the Augusteum.'

'Hey. You had a better few days than I did. What else?'

'It wasn't that good without you. I saw a cathedral that was damaged during the civil war…'

'Civil war?' Juliana asked.

'The Spanish Civil War. In the thirties. And a couple of other museums. They were really well laid out.'

'What were they called?'

'Haven't got a clue. They were good though.'

'There was a Civil War museum too. It is built on the galleries that were air-raid shelters during the war.'

Mike had a flash of memory. 'And a submarine,' he added.

'What about the submarine?' Charlotte prompted.

'They've got a submarine from over a hundred years ago. The Peral submarine I think was called. One of the first submarines ever used.'

They chatted on for a time about the submarine. Mike tried to concentrate, but he had to get away from this because his knowledge was a bit thin, and he knew he wasn't concentrating.

Then Juliana told stories of her time visiting her friends. They had apparently spent most of their time lazing about on the beaches, and having meals and drinks in the evening. Mike sometimes got the impression that she was not revealing everything, but he didn't question. Partly because he was sure she would not have stepped too far away from what he would have approved of, partly of course because he had done exactly that, and mostly because he didn't want the question of secrets being kept to come up. He knew his own secrets would be the worst of them all, and better kept silent.

So, he kept silent. Joined in as enthusiastically as he could, but didn't push anything.

In his own mind he kept thinking about what had happened. He could see Stephen as he fell, and the blood spreading all over his chest. He heard Maria telling him that they would part and not be together. Sometimes he thought they would get back together in a year or maybe two. Other times he thought they would never be together again. Sometimes, when he concentrated, he knew – knew – that he had lost her and they would not be together again.

Other times he thought about what was happening now, He had constant images of the police knocking on his door - or knocking it down! – and being taken away because they had forced Maria to admit, or they had found photos that linked the two of them. Sometimes he thought the people who had come over the top of the Penon just after Stephen had fallen would suddenly remember what they had seen and would describe him to the police. Those thoughts came to him now and again, randomly and inconveniently. But nothing happened. He was tied and perhaps a little drunk and Juliana cheerfully left him to that. Mike told her about a few of the restaurants he had eaten in. 'It will be nice to eat in them with someone; it will be better than eating alone.' He described where he had bought ice creams and coffees, and he told long and fictitious stories about his times lazing on the beaches.

'Did you climb up the Rock?' asked Juliana.

'Not really,' Mike replied, trying to get his thinking in order quickly. 'I walked up to the tunnel to have a look but no further.'

'Good,' said Juliana. 'That's a target then. We've got to do that. It's in all the guidebooks. We're the young and fit people that are supposed to do it.'

'I'm not sure I want to.' Mike shrugged, tried to reject the idea as pointless.

'Are you getting windy Mike old boy,' laughed Juliana. 'I'm going up there and I'm dragging you up with me if I have to chain you to my ankles,'

Mike joined in the laughter. But he was already planning ways to let that pass by.

Calpe 2023

Mike was in the fields behind the sea road, quite near to the salt flats, and they had planted strong smelling, perfumed, flowers to deaden the smells. He was walking through the flowers and smelling the beautiful, strong, pungent smells but also the faint smell of salt flats that had a tangy, less pleasant, scent.

Juliana could also have been smelling the same smells, but if she was, she didn't react to it. Mike couldn't be sure but he thought she was occupied, or concerned, with something else. They hadn't talked about much, but she was colder and more inwardly thinking than she had been.

'What are you thinking about?' Mike asked her, for the second time.

She stopped and looked up, as if she hadn't seen him before. 'Nothing.'

'No one thinks of nothing. You must be thinking of something.'

'I'm not.'

'The washing up. The next meal. The last meal. Your smelly knickers …'

She laughed as he did. 'Shut up, you horrible little man.'

'Ah. Welcome back to Planet Earth.' Mike relaxed slightly. 'Tell me the first word that comes to your mind.'

She ignored that. 'I was thinking about the letters and notes that Phil showed me. They were personal. It seems a bit strange to have read them. Like I could hear her talking to me, telling me things, that I know she wouldn't have told me in real life. I felt like I was intruding.'

'She's dead, Jooles. And it means something to her daughter to share it apparently. So that makes it okay.'

'Does it?' She thought about it for a while. 'Maybe it does. Or maybe not. I can feel both thoughts about it.'

'You can't hurt her. She's gone. You can help her daughter maybe.'

Juliana seemed to think about that a while, but said nothing directly.

'Phil wants to know who her lover was.'

Mike wasn't looking at her, but he could feel her looking at him as he thought through his reply. 'Does it matter now? It's a long time ago.'

'That's what I said. And in a way, she agrees. But I think she just wants to piece together everything she can about their lives. She just wants to know all she can.'

'Well, we can't help her there.'

'I know I can't. I wasn't around during that time anyway; when I got back everything had happened and I just picked up the story. It was pretty shocking I must admit.'

'Yeah.'

'Which just leaves you …'

'Well, I don't know who he was. I hardly saw Maria that week.'

'But you did see her during that week.' Juliana seemed to be fishing. 'Did you see her with anyone else?'

'I didn't see her at all.'

'You said you hardly saw her …'

'Yes, okay. All I mean is I saw her in town a couple of times and we exchanged hellos now and again. We had a coffee, I think, on one occasion.'

'But you never saw her with anyone else?'

'Never. I've said that all along. If she was with anyone then I don't know about it.'

They reached the edge of the plants and they climbed over a three of four brick-high wall onto the pavement, walked across the road and down a long, wide, passageway to the sea front. They were silent for a while.

'If she wrote those notes and letters did she not once say who she was talking about?' Mike tried to stay casual as he asked.

'No. Phil poured through every word of them. No names. No nicknames. Not even any description.'

'Huh.'

'It was as if,' Juliana went on 'she wanted to remind herself of her time together, with him, but was careful not to say who he was.'

'Okay. That sounds credible enough. She was with Stephen after all; she wouldn't want to tell him who she was with.'

'That doesn't follow. Probably when she wrote them he was already dead. But even if he wasn't, even if she was writing them each day when she was with her lover, the fact that she wrote them at all meant she risked him reading them. The fact that she was having an affair was the danger surely? Not who she was with?'

'I suppose.'

'So, what does that mean?' Juliana was looking straight at Mike.

'I don't know. What do you think it means?'

'I'm not sure. If I had to guess I'd say there was some reason for keeping his name out of it that we're not thinking about.'

They walked quietly for a while. Mike was sure that Juliana was thinking he was the guilty party. He was thinking he needed to deflect that thought, but he really had no idea how to do it without raising the whole subject again, and he didn't want to. Though he knew it had not gone away.

'I wondered if the shopping could give any clues. What they ate, drank.'

That sounded safer. 'Maybe. But it all seemed very basic the way you described it.'

'Yes. And the trips they took; I guess anyone could have done those. Sort of touristy stuff I suppose.'

'Yes.'

Juliana turned towards him as they continued slowly walking. 'You did know her. Of all the people here you're probably the one person she did know. I'm surprised you didn't see more of each other.'

Mike shook his head. 'I didn't know her that much. It was years ago, in the gym. I helped her do a cycle ride she wanted to do. It's not much of a connection.'

Juliana said nothing.

'And she came down here quite often. She probably knew a good many people we have no idea about. This was her territory, not ours.'

Juliana brightened up and flicked her head as if getting the past out of it. 'That is very true. It must be someone from here anyway. And it's Phil's problem.'

Calpe 2023

Mike did not know that Phil was invited to join them, but join them she did. Juliana was careful and watchful.

But Mike was worried.

Juliana poured Phil a glass of wine, Mike poured his own glass of scotch. He was watching Phil closely. As far as he could tell she was pleasant and calm, but all Mike could remember was Juliana's suggestion that Phil was checking to see who her father might be. Juliana didn't know where that road could lead, or at least she hoped she didn't, but Mike knew full well that it could lead to him.

He didn't believe that at all. He couldn't get his head round it, but he didn't think that Maria could have got pregnant in the days they had been together. It wasn't impossible obviously, but he felt so sure that would not be the case.

He was still trying to get his thinking straight when Phil threw him.

'You were the only person here in Calpe when my mother was here,' she said.

'Jooles,' gestured Mike, 'was close.'

'I am concerned that you and my mother were engaged in a relationship at that time. I know that she was seeing someone; her letters and diaries prove that. I think it was you.'

'Just a minute Phil. What you're saying accuses me of something ... wrongly ... and also drives an accusation between me and my wife. You have no right to do that.'

Phil was about to respond, but she looked at Juliana as if in question.

'Phil asked me about it,' said Juliana. 'I said she should say what she wanted to say. In front of us both.' Juliana stood up, and walked into the centre of the group. 'I expect you to show her, or prove, that you were not together with her. But I don't want this hidden in the dark. I want it out, exposed, and put aside so that you and I can get on with our lives, and so that Phil can also get on with hers.'

Mike was forced to nod, though feeling bitter and frightened. 'Okay. So, what makes you think Maria had a relationship, and that it was with me?'

Phil sat back. 'I have shown my mother's notes to Juliana. There is no question about her having an affair. She agrees with me on that. And if that person was you then I would like to know. But not just because I want to know. It was a long time ago; and I have no problem that she had relationships. No. My question is …. '

'Is that person your father …?' concluded Mike.

'No.' Phil was quite certain in the way she said that. 'No. I am my father's child. I have already had DNA tests that show that Stephen was my father. That is not an issue.'

Mike should have felt more relaxed hearing that, but he absolutely didn't. There was something else. And he wasn't quick enough to get there first.

'What I am interested in is whether her lover, you or someone else, killed my father. I think someone did, and I want to know why.'

Mike felt as if he had been hit in the face by a very hard fist. He sat down, and back in a chair as gracefully as he could, but he felt that he was falling backwards. Should he explain what he knew happened, but that would mean he had to admit it was him. Or should he deny knowing anything, in which case he would look like he was lying. And if Phil could prove it was him then she would also have him proven a liar, and that was not going to be a good place for him to deny murder from.

'I got this from the police.' Phil put a photo down on the table. 'It's a photo from a tourist just away from the Penon. That is definitely my mother in the photo, her clothes match several other photos I have of her. And that figure next to her looks a lot like you.'

Mike felt slightly relaxed. If that was the best Phil had, this wasn't going far. 'That could be almost anyone on the planet. You can't see his face, his hair style. Anything. I couldn't tell if that was me even if it was, and I can tell you it isn't, but even I couldn't identify myself from that. That's what you're hanging this on?'

Before Phil could answer Juliana, who had been looking over their shoulders, intervened. 'I'd have to agree. To be fair, I couldn't tell from that picture if that guy was him. That could be one of a million people.'

Phil nodded. 'I agree in fact.' She was going to pass on, but Juliana interrupted.

'Where did you get that from?'

'The police, as I said.'

'That photo was taken forty years ago. By a tourist, I would think. I don't know the law in this country for sure, but I think they have to destroy images like that within a month or so. How the hell do you have it?'

'The police kept this on file from the time of my father's death. They shared it with me a while ago.'

'When?'

'When they re-opened the case. When I asked them to re-open the case, and they did.'

Mike could feel sweat on the back of his neck; he hoped that wasn't showing.

Phil waited for a reply, but nothing came. 'I spoke to the owner of Vela en la Cueva, the restaurant on the front down there. He knew my mother, and he remembered her coming in a couple of times with a friend.'

'What? And after forty years he described me perfectly?'

Even Phil laughed slightly. 'No. He didn't remember what the friend looked like. And if he had I wouldn't have trusted him. It's been a long time. He did give me a bill though and apparently it was of a table booked by my mother, but signed off by a somewhat obscure name, not her. I could ask you for your signature to compare it to. But maybe that's not fair.'

Mike said nothing.

Phil threw down another photo. 'But that is definitely you. And that picture of you looks a hell of a lot like the guy in the first picture.'

'Well, I was here. But Maria isn't in this photo so what the hell does that prove.'

'Well, the clothes look similar. But you're right that we can't tie them up that closely. I can't prove that you were her lover on these.'

Mike listened carefully to what wasn't said. He wondered about the 'on these'. Was there more, or was this going to nowhere? Mike didn't ask, and nothing was said, about the fact that a photo of him, alone, had been saved for forty years by the police as part of a criminal investigation.

Phil relaxed and sat back. 'That's more or less all I have,' she said.

'I don't mean to be rude, but it doesn't sound like much. And nor would I expect it to be much after forty years. But the man you're looking for isn't me. You either have to find someone else, or put it aside and get on with your life.

'Can I remind you that Maria might, or might not, have had some reason for an affair but I was here with my girlfriend. And that girlfriend is sitting right here now. My wife. You trying to pull me into this is threatening my relationship with my wife. If I needed a reason other than you being wrong about this that would be a good reason to ask you to either put up or shut up.'

'Perhaps so.' Phil took another drink. She could see that Mike was not feeling easy. They shifted to chatting easily about Calpe today, the weather and the changes to the Penon and the rules for climbing it.

Calpe 1984

Juliana bought drinks out to the balcony, and came back balancing three bowls of different types of crisps.

Mike looked up from the book he was reading. 'What time is she coming over?'

'Anytime now,' Juliana said. 'She said she's got something very important to tell us.'

That's probably putting it mildly, thought Mike.

'How is she?' Mike grabbed some crisps and munched them.

'I think she's fine.' Juliana sat down with her drink. 'I called her and she said she'd pop over. She didn't sound quite right I must admit. A little quiet. But I think she's fine.'

They drank and munched for a while, and then there was a knock on the door and Juliana walked over and opened the door. She didn't come back to the balcony for quite a time and Mike stayed on the balcony, glancing at the magazine he had been reading. Mike kept an eye on the room, but it was bright on the balcony and that was throwing the room into shadow. He tried to see what was happening in the room, but he couldn't see either Juliana or Maria. He could vaguely hear them talking, but couldn't make out any words. He could tell they were talking more quietly than usual.

After a while he expected Juliana to come back alone; that Maria would have told her the story and then left, leaving it to Juliana to tell the story to him. But the two of them walked through to the balcony and Juliana carried with her a spare chair that she put down around the table and motioned to Maria to sit down.

They said their 'hellos' and raised glasses. Juliana looked over to Mike slightly, and then spoke. 'Maria has had an extraordinary few days,' she said. 'And none of them good. She's going back to the UK in a couple of days, but she wanted to drop in and speak to us first.'

Mike quietened, and slightly turned to face her. She seemed embarrassed but started boldly.

'My boyfriend died a couple of days ago,' she said. 'He fell off the Rock over there. I've been with the police, the Guardia, most of the last couple of days. You wouldn't believe all the stuff they need to know.'

'Christ.' Mike swigged down his drink. 'What the hell happened?'

'Well, they say he slipped while he was walking up there. There are some treacherous tracks up there, and a lot of warnings. Apparently, they have an accident up there every now and again. Some fatal.'

'So, he just slipped off?'

Maria paused for a moment. 'The police think there was more to it than that.' She didn't wait to be asked. 'He was wounded by a gunshot, and they are sure that will have had something to do with his fall.'

'He was shot?' Mike did his best to look shocked. 'Did he fall or was it … more … sinister?'

Maria shook her head. 'No. Not exactly. The bullet was from his own gun. Don't even ask me what that was about; I didn't even know he owned one, let alone that he was carrying it around here on holiday …'

'Or taking it on a climb like that. Why would he?'

'I have no idea. Apparently, the police think he may have had it with him to show off with; maybe shoot some birds or something. Anyway, it seems either he somehow shot himself, or the gun went off in his pocket when he started to fall. They're not sure.'

'Christ. That's awful.'

'Is that what they're thinking?' Mike asked.

'Yes. They're holding as possible that he got into a 'rage', and argument, with someone and he might have pulled the gun out to threaten someone and then triggered the gun somehow, but I can't believe that, and the police have nothing to support it.'

'Witnesses?'

'No. No-one saw what happened, or saw anyone in a fight or anything. I think they're keeping that possibility in their minds in case anything comes to light. But they seemed to have settled on just an accident on his own.'

Mike said how sorry he was. It brought tears to Maria's eyes, which even Mike thought were genuine.

'Is having a gun legal?' asked Juliana.

'No.' Maria was still looking down as she answered. 'It isn't. He shouldn't have had it. It was stupid. And it's turned into something awful.'

They all sat in silence for a bit.

'You have to have a licence for a gun. They give them to people who can prove they're vulnerable. Jewellers. Politicians. Footballers apparently too. He had no licence, just got a black-market gun for God knows what reason.'

That brought silence. It was something that hadn't been discussed and as far as Mike could tell Maria looked as if she hadn't thought of that either. But it also seemed unlikely that the Spanish police hadn't asked that question. It seemed unlikely that he could have brought it over from the UK, so he had probably bought it here. But why? Why in fact did he want a gun at all?

Maria shrugged. 'I've no idea. Maybe he did smuggle it in. Or maybe he bought it here. He knows … knew … a lot of people. I guess he could have got it over here somewhere.'

'But why?'

Maria shook her head. 'No idea. Something like that makes you realise that you don't know someone as much as you thought you did.'

Juliana waved her hands to stop it all. 'Come on. Let's leave it. It's terrible enough for Maria without digging it all out. Let's leave it.'

The two of them quietly nodded.

Juliana went on. 'It will all come out in the end.'

Calpe 2023

It was the following day that Mike thought more deeply about the implications. Juliana was back at their villa, and he had told her he was just going out and might even climb the Penon.

'Do you want me to come with you?'

Mike shook his head. 'No, I just want to wander about for a bit. I probably won't be long. And if I do go up the Penon I'm told its dangerous so I'd rather see it without you. At first at least.'

'Okay. Take care. And given the choice I'd say don't climb the damn thing.'

Mike left and walked towards the centre. He was pretty sure that Phil knew that he, Mike, had been with her mother and in an intimate way. Yet she had left the day before without any obvious animosity, and she had seemed to respect Mike's privacy about that intimacy by not revealing it to Juliana. Juliana could hardly be unaware of that possibility, and Mike knew that there would be questions and repercussions later, but at the moment he had enough on his plate.

Mike walked into a café on the front, ordered a coffee and sat back and looked at the Penon in front of him.

Climb.

Mike checked the text on his phone. He looked to see who had sent it, but there was no source number. Mike didn't even know you could do that. He thought you had to give away your own number. Straight away, that alarmed him. He wondered for a while if he could find out from someone, his provider perhaps, who had sent the message.

He could see now that walk up the Penon forty years ago. He looked up the road to where a small restaurant used to be, at least as he remembered it. And he remembered getting ice creams for the two of them there. Then he looked back to the Penon, and he remembered that sense that he had had back then when he was walking towards it that a mass of other people had been walking towards it. And he had felt like he was one of them. That they all shared a sense of purpose. As he had walked towards the Penon he felt a part of a larger group all with one purpose. It had been a good feeling, and to be honest, a rare feeling to be part of a larger group with a common purpose.

He stood up and walked towards the Penon, slowly and drifting there without purpose. As he walked, he looked towards the road to the side where he remembered the start of the walk was. He even smiled as he remembered back then that he and Maria hadn't even been able to find the right starting point. It made him feel young then, and grown-up now.

For a while it was very pedestrian. Left and right on a well-crafted path through the climbing grass and shrubs, up to an area that was obviously an entrance site where you paid your fee to make the climb, or could buy snacks and drinks before you went on. None of this had been there forty years ago. But in fact there was no-one there and nothing in the vending machines against the walls. He walked through a revolving turnstile, again with no-one there. He had no idea if the arrangement was a new set up that had not yet been opened, or that he was there off-season and nobody manned the place at that time of the year. He looked for anywhere where he could contribute some fees voluntarily, but there wasn't even anywhere for that. He decided that he would put some money in a charity box in the town later.

When he got to the tunnel he had noticed that the walk so far had been very different to the walk forty years ago. More modern, more structured. But now in the tunnel it was if he had passed backwards in time; he was here now and he had been there then and there was no difference.

On the other side of the tunnel, as he emerged into the sunlight, and now on the northern side of the Penon, he looked up the winding paths ahead of him, and at the groups of people plodding along the various routes. He decided to stop, and go back down and get something to eat. He turned and started towards the tunnel.

And that was when his phone signalled that he had just received another text.

Where are you? it said.

He texted back. *Who is this?*

Where are you?

Calpe

So am I. Where are you?

He wondered for a moment if it could be Juliana and that the anonymity was just some accident in the way she had sent the message.

But he realised immediately they had texted each other many times and this had never happened.

Where are you?

In a café. In the old own. Where are you?

There was a delay before the next text came in. *I am on the Penon de Ifach*

He thought about that for a moment. He even looked around to see if Juliana, or anyone else, was punching their phone in front of him, but he couldn't see anybody doing that although he knew a lot of people somewhere there would be doing just that. But the rest of the message then came in. *And so are you*

Who the fuck are you?

No answer. But he was sure he knew. Who else could be sending threatening-sounding texts to him. He guessed that Phil was somewhere on the Penon, probably ahead of him. And playing with him.

He looked around, but couldn't see her. But it was a déjà vu again; it reminded him of being on the Penon forty years ago and finding Stephen up there near him. Threatening him.

He decided to go on. He wanted to confront Phil and ask her to stop threatening him. Whatever she thought he knew, he wanted to change her mind about it, calm her down. He saw them becoming friends. Well, why not? But he also knew why not. He might pull it off, but if he did it would be based on a lie.

Yes, come to me, the next text said.

So, wherever Phil was she could see him. He looked carefully along the edges of the cliffs above him, and looked all around him, but he could see nothing. He knew, though, that if she was far enough away and concealed that she could hide for a long time. He kept on walking.

Where are you? he texted. But he got no reply.

He walked a bit further. Soon he came to the area where forty years ago he had come down from the Penon. He consciously avoided it, and turned onto an easier path back above where he had just been walking. All the time he was keeping an eye out for signs of Phil.

There were people occasionally in view, and he checked each one out but none looked like Phil or seemed to be acting in any way secretively.

Where are you? he texted again.

After he had received no reply again he added *We should get together*

We will.

Mike stared at the reply with a sense of fear; it didn't have to be a threat but he was damned sure it was.

He turned again, did a small climb up the area where the rusty chains were there to assist, and turned yet again. Gradually he was making his way to the top of the Penon's main body. Even if he reached it, there was still a very long climb along the brow of the hill to the highest point where it overlooked the town below. If he had to climb it he would, but he hoped not to have to.

He stopped on a prominent area where he could get a wide angled look around the Penon. Slowly he turned around keeping an eye out for Phil. He didn't know what she would be wearing but he thought he would be able to pick her out once he could see her.

Nothing happened. No texts. No sight of Phil.

So, Mike stopped and stood still. He held his phone in his hand, but down by his side. He would play the classic game of 'who blinks first'.

Keep coming.

Mike felt a stupid sense of victory because he had forced Phil to call out first. He turned towards the peak, and he could see dozens of people at different points along the Penon, and many up at the very peak, most of those having their photo-moment at the concrete post that had been inserted into the rocks above the view of the town.

Keep coming.

Mike kept slowly climbing, but he didn't text any replies.

He climbed for another fifteen minutes, in silence, and slowly. With virtually every step he checked around for Phil, and he kept an eye on his own position to ensure he always knew his best way down and out of the position.

And then he saw Phil

She was sitting on a rock, her back to higher rocks, drinking from a plastic bottle and watching him approach. She was in a vulnerable position providing she stayed sitting, and Mike walked carefully towards her.

Phil waved to him and beckoned him over. Mike automatically waved back, feeling slightly surrealistic. Phil stayed sitting, Mike stayed standing.

There was an awkward moment while they both stood looking at each other. Mike was about to speak, but Phil got in first.

'It's a bit of a coincidence meeting you up here.'

Mike thought it must be laced with sarcasm, but everything about Phil's face was innocent. Plain. Simple 'Yes.' He thought a bit. 'I had no plan to be here, just decided to walk up. I haven't done that for a long time.'

'Forty years?'

'Yes. It was easier in those days. I was fitter and younger. Or this hill's getting tougher.'

Phil laughed.

Mike wearied about the whole situation. It was decades ago. He was tired. Tired of thinking about it and arguing about it. So Phil knew that he had had an affair with her mother forty years ago, and she knew that he wasn't her father. Her father had died, but he had been clear to Maria at the time, and Phil now, that he hadn't been responsible for that. It was suddenly very clear to him that this was a pointless argument and he wanted to end it now. Make it clear, and leave the Penon, hopefully at ease with each other.

'Phil,' he started, 'we both know that I was here with your mother forty years ago. We had a brief affair and it ended when it happened. Is that such a dreadful thing to remember?'

'Not at all.'

Mike shrugged. Flicked out his arms dismissively.

'It's troubled me for a long time that my father died here too though. I've spent a lifetime worrying that he might have been killed.'

'By me?'

'By anyone,' Phil answered. 'The police, my mother, everyone accepted that it was an accident. But it's troubled me all my life.'

'And what do you want to do about it?

'Accept it. I've been poking around here for ages, and worrying for longer, and I've found nothing to suggest anything. I can spend the rest of my life worrying about it, and die not knowing.' She looked down, shaking her head. 'It's time to accept it.'

Mike was relieved. Very relieved. He relaxed. 'I'm glad. I must admit that I was worried when I got your texts that you were trying to threaten me, or something like that. Your texts sounded sinister. I'm glad we can shake hands on it and walk away.'

'What texts?'

'The texts you've been sending me for the past hour or so.' Mike held out his phone. Phil just shook her head, apparently genuinely puzzled. Mike flicked the phone on, and showed her the texts they had been exchanging on the Penon.

'That's not me,' Phil said.

Calpe 2023

Phil leaned forward and took the phone Mike was pointing at her. She looked at the texts on screen, looked up at Mike to seek silent permission to check further, which he got, and she scanned through the texts, checking them. She handed back the phone. 'That's not me,' was all she repeated.

'Well, if not you then who sent this?'

Phil turned up the corners of her mouth and shook her head. 'Whoever this is says he, or she, is up here on the Penon with us.'

Mike was clearly unconvinced, but they both looked around. There were a few people within a reasonable distance, and a few more a bit further away, but no-one obviously looking at them.

They both thought quietly for a time, but there seemed no obvious way forward.

'Where did you get the stuff from, the stuff that told you I was with your mother,' Mike asked. 'Did your mother give it to you?'

Phil nodded. 'Some of it. I found papers around our house, years ago some of them. And Mama didn't exactly deny it, though she would never mention names or any really useful details.'

Mike shrugged, and set back to thinking. Phil didn't though. 'Not all of it I'll admit. Some of it was sent to me at the house a while after Mama died. Nothing very different, just more of the same, maybe a little more detail about where you had been.'

'Who sent it?'

'Well actually Mama I think. It came from her bank and they refused to tell me where they had got it from. Said it was confidential. They were instructed to send it to me and I imagine it was a package Mama had stored there and asked them to send to me if she died.'

'But it didn't say anything much you didn't already know?'

'No, not really.'

'Suppose it was someone who didn't know you already knew most of it. Maybe someone who thought they were revealing it to you for the first time? Would that make sense?'

'It would. But there isn't anyone I can think of.'

They lapsed into silence again.

'What do you want Phil? Do you want to punish me? Get something from me? What?'

Phil shook her head. 'No. If I wanted to punish you I could have pressed harder with your wife. I'm passed that point. A long time ago, really.'

Mike stayed silent.

'What would be the point of that? You and Mama were grown up and you did what you did. It doesn't hurt me to think of it anymore. I don't want to cause trouble for you or your family and friends. I've got all I want. I know about my dad. And I've got to move on now. Get on with my life. I think it's time to just put it behind me.'

'That's very sensible. Very real. It's very mature. I admire you, I truly do.'

Phil nodded.

'But someone doesn't feel like that. Someone is following me up here. And if that wasn't you, who was it?'

'I hate to say it but I'm guessing it comes from your side,' Phil admitted. 'Your wife perhaps. I've spoken to her as part of my looking at all this, and I've tried to be as discreet as I could be in the circumstances, but maybe she's put it all together. There were things I had to ask. Maybe she had something neither of us knows about that has told her something? Is that possible?'

Mike shook his head. 'I think I know who this might be. Do you know someone called Purdey?'

Phil shook her head. 'No. Never heard the name.'

Mike decided to lay it on the line. 'I am being blackmailed, rather childishly to be frank, by a girl called Purdey. She has knowledge that your mother and I had an affair as well. I assumed you must have been in touch with her at the very least.'

Phil was very adamant when she shook her head again.

'I think it's me you're looking for?' The voice came from behind them.

Mike turned, and looked around the few people standing nearby. The woman standing fairly close was taking a scarf from around her head, exposing herself more clearly.

It was Purdey.

Mike looked towards Phil, expecting that this was the time they would own up and show their allegiance. But Phil's lips were turned down, and she was still shaking her head.

'Let me tell you who you are first,' she said. 'You're the fucking bastard who killed my father.'

Mike really tried to grasp that, but nothing came together. 'I think you're somehow on the wrong story lady.'

'You killed my father. Stephen. You murdered him.'

Phil was quietly watching both of them. Mike hoped she could genuinely see just how puzzled, and shocked, he was.

It was Phil who spoke first. 'If you're meaning my father, I don't believe he was murdered.'

'Yes, he was.' She pointed at Mike. 'That cunt shot him and threw him off the cliff.'

Mike faced her square on. 'You're talking crap. I don't know who you are, but you obviously know nothing about this. You say you're Stephen's daughter.' Mike turned towards Phil. 'Do you have a sister? Jooles only mentioned you had a brother. Charlie. But he's dead.'

Phil was looking very disturbed. 'Charlie was a girl, my sister. And no, she isn't dead though that is what I told your wife. It is a family … secret … I suppose. She is safely locked up. In an asylum. You can't be Charlie.'

The woman took a photo out of her pocket and showed it to Phil, but she seemed unimpressed.

'Okay. This is a picture of my mother with a child, but no one I recognise. What is this supposed to prove?'

'So why am I carrying this about?'

'My guess,' said Phil, 'is that you got the photo somewhere and you're playing a game. If you're my sister where have you been for … well, all of my life? I understand you've been locked up.'

'I've been ill. I've been hospitalised for many years. I only got released a while ago and I've been trying to catch up. That's when all this came to light.'

Phil was thinking about it, but Mike jumped it. 'If you were hospitalised then presumably your mother visited you often, or sometimes at least. What do you mean that you had to catch up. That it all 'came to light'. That doesn't make sense.'

Mike tried to calm down the moment. If you are Charlie, then why have you been using the name Purdey. Are you sure Purdey isn't actually your real name, and you're … confused … about your identity?'

Purdey smiled. 'A personal joke. I loved the programme called the Avengers, or the New Avengers in fact. Joanna Lumley was taken on to play the female role and she was given the name `Charlie'. She herself changed it to Purdey for the role. I loved that program and I loved Purdey. I decided to become Purdey, just as she had done.'

Mike had nothing to say, and looked at Phil for support.

'That rings a bell from my childhood,' she replied. 'Something about that.' She hesitated, 'She might be my sister.'

But Charlie's face became red with anger. 'They kept me away from my mother and my sister for years. Decades. The hospicio kept me away from her.'

Phil stood up. 'Hospicio?' she said. 'Hospicio or Manicomio?'

The woman made a fierce and rude gesture to Phil and then to Mike. 'Whatever you want to call it. Our mother imprisoned me there.'

Phil turned to Mike. 'It's just possible. This fits with things I heard in my family over time.'

'This is your sister?'

'Possibly.'

'And she's been in hospital all this time.'

Phil shook his head. 'Manicomio. What do you call it? Institution? Madhouse?'

'An asylum?' Mike asked.

'Yes. An asylum.'

Mike said rudely 'Sounds like she should still be in one.'

But the woman didn't react as he might have expected. 'I fucking would be if I hadn't discharged myself. I could have spent my whole life there.'

'Discharged yourself?' Phil asked.

'Call it what you like. I'm out now. And I want revenge for what you did to my father'

Phil seemed to take charge. She was getting the picture, and understanding that the problem was, at least largely, hers.

'Whatever happened, he didn't do anything. How can you think he did?'

'I was fucking delighted to know my mother and father were happy. But then she met you.' She dismissively thrust a hand towards Mike. 'And you stole her away from Dad. She fell head over heels in love with you and rejected Dad.'

'What are you talking about? Mike was with someone else and they stayed together and Mum would have probably stayed with Dad if the accident hadn't happened.' Phil was trying to swim through the treacle Purdey was building up.

'Dad and Mum were doomed because this bastard killed him. He shot Dad on that fucking mountain and pushed him off to his death.'

'That's bollocks,' was Mike's sudden reaction.

'And what do you think Mama's reaction was when she found that out?'

'This is garbage.'

'She killed herself. She took her own life rather than live with the knowledge that her one-night stand had killed her lover. She took a drug overdose and then you – you, Phil – conspired with the family to cover that up and pretend it was a cancer that had killed her.'

'You're off with the fairies.' Phil had stitched a puzzled expression permanently on her face.

'And you too, you cunt.' She pointed directly at Mike. 'I know that Dad could be a violent man. But she loved him despite that. Then you came along and she fell in love with you. You persuaded her that he was a bad man.'

Mike held his hands out in surrender. He wanted to find some way to calm down the atmosphere and bring some sanity to what was, clearly, anything but.

'Don't fucking come near me,' Purdey screamed. And she started to back away. It took a while before both Mike and Phil realised she was leaving them. She was walking away, and towards the downward path.

'Where are you going?' Phil called.

'I will get the both of you. I will get the both of you for what you have done.'

Mike started to call out that 'no-one had done anything' but Phil stopped him. 'Leave her. She's obviously very ill. I don't think Dad was killed, and I know for sure that Mum died of cancer. This girl is very disturbed.'

'She's very dangerous,' exclaimed Mike. 'To herself mainly, and possibly to you and me, and just possibly everyone around here. She's nuts.'

'She is insane. But what can she do? In the end she can only shout. My mother died of cancer. I should know that, I was with her all the time. Perhaps Charlie, if this is her, will also come to see that. One way or the other this will not last long. When we are back on the ground I will call the hospital and they will find her and take her back. Then perhaps I can do something more practical to help her. I am not very rich but my mother left me enough to be very comfortable with. I can use some of the money to help her. It may take time, but I owe that to my mother.'

'What would your mother be thinking? Now? About this? If she was alive, would she agree with you?'

'I think so. But that doesn't matter; she is not still alive. It is my duty now to help my family. And it seems that this lady could well be my sister. I will deal with the hospital to help her.'

'I'd call the police too,' Mike said. 'I think she sounds dangerous.'

'To herself perhaps.' Phil made gestures that were clearly taking control of the situation from Mike. Mike did feel a need to help; crazy though Purdey was to blame him for Stephen's death - and Maria's death! - Mike had nonetheless had a relationship with her mother that might have helped push her over the edge of sanity. He felt the need to do what he needed to.

But Phil had seen that coming, and she was very clear. 'You must leave now,' she said.

'But…..'

'I am not just being polite. It is my job to deal with this. And let me be clearer, I have no cross to bear against you for what you and my Mama did. I have said that. But you are not part of my life and I don't want you to be. It has been useful to talk with you, but that is done now. It is time for us to part. As friends I hope. But part.'

Mike felt very different about it, but he knew that part of that was a re-awakened feeling for Maria, and he understood that in a way Phil felt that also. Phil was rejecting that and Mike had to accept it. He nodded, and said nothing more.

Mike started to walk away, and Phil held out her hand. Silently they shook hands, said nothing, and Mike walked away down the hill. He turned once, and saw Phil just standing quietly, watching him go.

Mike plodded down the hill, fairly slowly. He took time to make sure he was safe on the harder parts of the walk, and held tight to the chains where that was necessary. He knew that it was right that he leave; this was Phil's problem now and Phil had made clear that she knew that and expected that to be adhered to.

But Mike was sure that Phil was not going to find it that easy to discourage her sister. There were aspects to her that he had seen before; a disconnection with reality. He didn't know what to call it, but he had seen it in obsessives. He knew it as the 'ratchet-effect'; like a ratchet screwdriver turned in one direction tightened the screw, but turns in the opposite direction didn't loosen it, they just had no effect. Obsessives like her would keep strengthening her insane beliefs with everything that felt right to her, and other facts would just be ignored.

He looked around for either the sister or Phil, but he could see neither. He resolved that it was time to walk away. It really wasn't his problem.

Phil was still up at the top, sitting where she had been when Mike had first seen her. She was looking around like any tourist, but in fact seeing nothing outside her own head. She was thinking about how she could convince her sister, Charlie, that their parents' deaths were just a part of fate, and that no-one was to blame for them. She knew that would be difficult, but she also knew she had a duty to try.

The sister stood away from Phil, but looking at her.

Phil stood up. 'You are Charlie?'

The sister nodded.

'Let's go down. Go down there, get a coffee, and maybe something to eat. We have a lot to talk about.'

Charlie nodded again.

Soon they came together and, with Charlie slightly in the lead, they walked away from the peak down the first paths, and towards the centre of the Penon. Charlie seemed strong and safe on the walk, and rejected most of Phil's attempts to assist her. Eventually she gave up and walked behind her as they moved slowly down the slopes.

Mike was concentrating on the sister – Purdey, or Charlie - as he walked down the steps. He knew she felt antagonistic towards him. He knew he'd done nothing wrong, but maybe that wasn't the point. Why did she just let him walk away? Was she going to track him down later? Did she want Phil to think she had forgotten him and then come back and get him later? She had called him a 'fucking bastard' who had killed her Dad, and indeed her Mum .… that sounded pretty aggressive.

And she had said she wanted revenge. Clearly the earlier blackmail had been part of a ruse to find and deal with him, Mike understood. Mike wondered for a moment if perhaps she was actually working with Phil to get to him. But almost as he thought it, he dismissed it; he was as certain as he could be that Phil was as surprised as he had been about this sister.

Just what was going on in her head? Mike knew that whatever it was it probably wasn't very ordered or logical.

Phil was up near Charlie when she started talking again.

'What do you want to do about this cocksucker?' she said, almost spitting,

'Charlie, I don't think we should think of it that way. Our parents just had a life that didn't involve us and we should let it go. It's not time to look backwards; we should both be looking forwards.'

Charlie stopped and turned to look directly at Phil. 'I don't have a future. And my past was ruined by that man. You have a duty, a duty to me, to help me sort that cunt out.'

'No. That's not the way forward.'

'It's my way forward. And if you're not with me then you're against me.'

'I'm not....'

'For me or against me,' she demanded. 'For me or against me.'

Mike saw the probable conclusion. Charlie was against him for his time with Maria and for what she thought he had done to Stephen. He was her target. So why was she with Phil? Mike knew that she was trying to get Phil on to her side; to come at him together. And if she succeeded would that satisfy her, or would she anyway then go after Phil?

Whatever the answer was to that he wanted to confront it now and get rid of it. He turned and walked back up the path to find and confront the sister, or possibly the two of them.

Red faced, and shouting almost incoherently, Charlie attacked Phil. She kicked, and she pulled and pushed her. In that instant Phil knew she was trying to push her off of the Penon. But she was strong enough to contain her anger, to stop her forcing her back. To make that even harder for her she backed herself against the Penon's wall and held her away. Trying to convince her.

She saw fast movement below, and saw that Mike was running back up the hill.

Mike saw the position, or thought he did. Phil pushed back against the wall and Charlie was about to spin her backwards and throw her off the side of the Penon. He could calm this down, and be part of reconciling this anger. He and Phil had got on well and they could work together.

Mike grabbed Charlie, sure of his stronger ground to that Phil was standing on. He tried to turn her.

He only had a short time to recognise how he had wrongly guessed the dynamics.

The sister – Phil called out the name 'Charlie' loudly – turned at full force and without restraint, grabbing Mike with a fierceness he hadn't expected.

He thought for a moment that he could hold the position for them both. But a part of his mind immediately switched to Juliana. She would not know what had happened to him. She might be able to work it out later, but at least at first she would be in mystery about it. He realised he was thinking about Juliana in an oblique sort of way, and that he had no doubts now that he loved her. That he had always loved her. He wanted her to know that, but in his last movement he knew that he could never tell her.

Locked together they span off a small tree behind him and the two of them flew off the Penon, and fell down the two-hundred-foot chasm towards the rocks in the sea below.